The LAST BEAR

Also by Hannah Gold:

The Lost Whale

The LAST BEAR

HANNAH GOLD

ILLUSTRATIONS BY KATE SLATER

HARPER

An Imprint of HarperCollinsPublishers

TO MY PARENTS, THE PLANET,
AND POLAR BEARS EVERYWHERE

★

SVALBARD
↑ 240 miles

BEAR
ISLAND

N
S

WALRUS
BAY

BEAR'S
CAVE

JAGGED
CLIFFS

GIGANTIC
BOULDERS

CABIN

NORWAY
250 miles

ARRIVAL

1

THE LETTER

APRIL WOOD CAME FACE-TO-FACE with the polar bear exactly three weeks after she had arrived on Bear Island. But before that, she had to get to Bear Island in the first place, and that journey began approximately four months earlier.

Up until that point, there had been a normality to April's everyday life, although she was the first to admit it was a rather odd kind of normality. Her father worked as a scientist in a nearby university, where he spent his days researching weather patterns. Like the weather, he came and left the house at the most unpredictable of times—sometimes he'd get home at eleven p.m. or he would leave just when she got home from school. He worked random weekends but would have three days off in the week. Even then he would shut himself in his study and bury his face in dusty old books with writing so tiny it made your eyes hurt just to read them. When April brought him a pot of tea or his dinner, he would shake his head, take off his glasses, and look at her curiously, as if he had completely forgotten he had a daughter. "Oh," he would say. "Thank you . . . April."

Then he would put his head back down and chew the top of his pen, and she would gently close the study door behind her.

April was only four when her mother died, and whenever she thought of her, it was like thinking of a lovely summer vacation she'd once been on. Her father hadn't remarried, and it showed in the house. It was tall and thin and looked ever so slightly unhappy around the edges, and inside it always felt cold. There was a thin layer of dust coating everything, and a horrible feeling of something missing—a feeling that April never quite knew how to put into words.

And so she spent most of her time in the backyard, where, in the wild, unkempt bramble bush, a family of urban foxes lived. She was fascinated by one in particular who she called Braveheart, because he seemed bolder than the others and because once he'd *almost* allowed her to feed him some strawberries from her hand. Time spent in the yard whizzed by and was only interrupted by school. April didn't like school, or the girls at the school didn't like her. She didn't know whether it was because she smelled of fox or the fact that she was the smallest girl in her class or even that she cut her own hair with a pair of garden shears. Either way, April didn't mind too much because she preferred animals to humans anyway. They were just kinder.

Then the letter arrived.

April was eating a bowl of cornflakes cross-legged on the floor while on the other side of the living room, her father dangled a piece of toast dripping with marmalade over today's newspaper. It was the end of November, and April raced to the door when the mail landed with a thud on the mat. Maybe it would be a Christmas card from Granny Apples? She not only liked to send her cards early but was also her favorite grandmother because she smelled of warm sugary pastry and lived next to the sea.

There were no Christmas cards, but there was a big fat envelope marked OFFICIAL GOVERNMENT BUSINESS and it was postmarked Norway.

She placed it by her father's toast, and he absentmindedly picked it up to take a bite. When he realized what it was, a funny look passed over his face, as if someone had cast a magic spell into his eyes.

"What is it?" she asked him.

"We're going to the Arctic Circle," he said, opening

the letter and blinking fast. "I got the job. I didn't think I would, to be honest—I thought they would choose someone local. But apparently my research paper on the scientific study of atmosphere swayed them. It's a weather station on a small island about a day's boat journey away from the coast of Norway."

April hopped up and down before answering. "What kind of island? How many people live there?"

"Ah." He looked down sheepishly. "It's not that kind of island. In fact . . . there won't be anyone there but us."

"Just us two?" Something fizzy rushed through her. "On an island all alone?"

He leaned forward in his chair. "Think of the adventures we will have. We'll be like Scott of the Antarctic. The island is nothing like here—it's got inland lakes, mountains, streams. Imagine it, April. It's the last great unknown. There'll be no cars, trains, planes. No roads even! It's pure, untouched wilderness."

He didn't need to say anything more, because her heart was already racing ahead. Not only would they be in the Arctic Circle, they would also have all this time together. Just them. They would be able to do so many things—like building snowmen, sledding down mountains, and—

"Of course, my work there will be very important," Dad added with his most serious face, and her insides crumpled the tiniest bit.

"What will you be doing?"

"The Norwegian government wants a more accurate representation of how global warming is affecting the Arctic region, so I'll be monitoring the data over a six-month period."

April knew a lot about melting ice caps, and along with fox hunting, it was one of the things that made her feel both angry and useless at the same time.

"And my school?" she asked.

"April," he said, leaning forward. "Six months in the Arctic will teach you more than six years at school ever will."

She took a second look at him. His eyes were bright, and there were two pink spots of color on his cheeks. The feeling fizzed through her again.

"When do we go?!"

Of course, not everyone was as excited. Granny Apples phoned at least three times a day to tell them how irresponsible they were being. What about the freezing cold temperatures, the waves as tall as skyscrapers, the killer walruses with sharp tusks she'd seen in one of those David Attenborough documentaries, or the dangers of an island where there was no hospital, no doctor, or even anybody else at all who could help them should they get into trouble.

It just wasn't right for a girl of eleven, she said. Especially such a sensitive girl as April who, thanks to her father, was feral enough already. How could he possibly think going away to a deserted island—and not even a warm one at that—was in her best interests?

But Dad was stubborn when he wanted to be and just pretended to be deaf.

"For goodness' sake, Edmund," she bellowed at him in frustration. "It's called Bear Island. What if she gets eaten?"

Although he tried to reassure her that there were no bears on Bear Island, Granny Apples refused to listen.

"If you see a polar bear, April," she said, "remember to RUN."

So it was that on April 1, they started the first leg of their journey. They were to fly to Oslo, then change planes and head to a small town called Tromsø—and from there a boat journey to Bear Island. As the plane took off and turned its nose north, April pressed her face to the window and looked down on her disappearing home.

This was it.

They were headed to the Arctic Circle.

2

BEAR ISLAND

"YOU KNOW your father is mad?"

April jumped at the sudden noise, bashing her elbow against the metal railing. The seagull she'd been feeding out of her hand with oat biscuit crumbs flew off with an indignant squawk. At her side was a boy she'd last heard swearing loudly dockside at Tromsø as he lifted Dad's entire Mozart collection and record player onto the slightly rusty Norwegian cargo ship they had found to take them to Bear Island. He was the captain's son and perhaps two or three years older than her. Up close, he smelled of brine and engine juice and something else she couldn't identify. But then again, everything had been different—wilder and emptier—since they'd left, so perhaps he didn't smell unusual at all.

But still. That didn't make his words acceptable, and they definitely didn't justify a reply. Not only that, she didn't trust herself to speak as the peanut butter sandwich she'd eaten earlier was perilously close to coming back up again.

"I would lie down if I were you," the boy instructed, and pointed to the bench that sat tucked under the bow. "It will help with the seasickness."

April looked at the hard wooden bench dubiously. But after another violent heave, she edged toward it and lay down so all she could see was sky. Tucked down here, she was at least shielded from the unrelenting wind that stung her face red raw. She expected the boy to disappear, but instead he sat quietly at the end of the bench and picked the dirt out from under his fingernails.

"He's not mad," she said when her stomach finally started to feel less queasy. "He's a *scientist*."

"That is even worse," the boy said, turning to face her.

"My father says the weather station on the island has been staffed since 1918."

"Yes! But not by a . . . girl."

"I don't know why you have to say 'girl' in that tone of voice." April sat up indignantly. "Just because I'm not a boy doesn't mean I'm weak. I once climbed the horse chestnut tree in our backyard right to the very top so I could rescue our next-door neighbor's cat!"

The boy didn't reply. Instead, he laughed one of those big belly laughs and spanned his arms to indicate the huge expanse of mottled sky, the rough tumbling seas, and the feeling like they weren't even on Earth at all. "What do you know about this part of the world?" he asked once he had finished laughing. "Have you ever been this far north?"

"I know you are a rude boy," said April. "And I know if I were in your shoes, I would be a lot more helpful about what to expect. Besides, I'm not scared of the unknown."

Something in his face softened. "Tör," he said, holding out his hand. "Don't mind us. My father and I spend so long at sea, we forget how to be human."

"April. April Wood."

She shook his hand. It felt like old rope but strangely comforting too. Like a hand that could pull her out of trouble.

"Is it dangerous?" she asked in a quiet voice.

"It is wild," said Tör. "And all wild things are dangerous."

"But there are no polar bears?"

Tör shook his head. "Not for years. But why the sad face? Polar bears are not friendly animals. They are not pets. They'll eat a girl like you alive."

April pretended to stare at the sea rather than look at his silly grin.

"I don't understand your trick with the seagull."

"What trick?" April turned back to face him.

"How you got it to eat out of your hand."

"It's not a trick," she said, bristling at the assumption. "I've just learned how to make animals feel safe with me."

Tör raised an eyebrow, but something in his face invited conversation.

"It's about listening to them," she explained, touching her heart. "Here."

"You're different," he said.

"So I'm not *just* a girl, then?"

Tör smiled, and it was such a wide-open smile that April couldn't help but grin back. "When you are on the island, you won't be able to leave. You know that, don't you?" he said, lowering his tone. "Not until we come in six months to pick you up."

April had the sense there was something else. She was clever at hiding the things she really wanted to say, especially around her father, and had a sixth sense for when someone else was doing the same. She waited for him to say it, because whatever it was, she would rather know. But in the end, he pulled out a pencil stub from his jacket and scrawled his number on the back of an envelope he had stuffed in his pocket.

"Bear Island is a hard place. You be careful, April Wood," he said. "And if you ever need me at all, just call this number."

She couldn't imagine why she would need him, but she tucked it into her coat pocket just in case. Then she watched as he rejoined his fellow crew members, who, with their strong sturdy limbs, weather-cracked hands, and stoic faces, made her father look like he was made of parchment. Since the ship had left port, he had shut himself into their cabin and surrounded himself with books to prepare himself for his new job. And because she knew he didn't want to be disturbed and because the cabin smelled of mackerel, she settled back down on the bench and fell asleep.

★

"Land ho!" The call echoed throughout the ship like the way a church bell calls out a wedding. "Land ho!"

April pulled herself upward, her head groggy with dreams, and then had to blink twice to make sure she was seeing correctly. Standing before her on deck was Tör, with his palm outstretched and a hunk of bread sitting on it. As he gazed skyward, his face carried the kind of hopeful expression she'd worn on her first day at school. Something in it made her lean toward him.

"You need to hold your body a bit lighter and stop holding your breath."

"Like this?" he asked as he dropped his shoulders and let his arm relax.

"More from the inside," April instructed. "As if you're made of water. How it's all soft and gentle. That's it. Nice and easy. Now don't move. He's right there above you. Quiet now and—"

"Tör!" the captain yelled across the deck, and the seagull squawked as it shot into the sky. April shied backward. She didn't know what to make of the captain, who was unlike anyone she'd ever met before. "I hope you're not distracting our guests," he said, taking a curious glance at the bread in Tör's hand. "We need your help at the bow."

Tör dropped the bread and ran off while April held her breath as the captain's gaze raked over her. There was something fierce in his face, as if he had gotten so used to the wild north seas, he had forgotten where he ended and they began. For once, she was glad of her height and the way it made her invisible.

Without another word, he strode away, and April

let out a long sigh of relief. Around her, the deck was busy with crew and their quick, efficient activity. She couldn't see Tör, but her father was impossible to miss. He was leaning over the bow of the ship, wearing his tweed jacket and pressed suit trousers—oblivious to the freezing temperatures—and staring in awe at the horizon. She edged closer to him, and even over the smell of the sea, she breathed in the familiar scent of the aniseed candy he liked to suck.

"Dad?"

"We're here, April! We're here!" he said, without breaking his gaze. "We've made it."

He pointed to something, but she couldn't see anything apart from sea spray, rolling gunmetal waves, and a sense they were entering a forbidden part of the universe.

"Isn't she beautiful?"

The island finally came into view, the way that you

spin the nozzle on the binoculars and suddenly things become clear and sharp.

"Bear Island," he said in a hushed voice full of awe and wonder.

A GIFT OF TIME

"THIS IS IT," said Dad, standing on the windswept beach surrounded by crates and suitcases and gazing around him. "What do you think?"

April's lips tasted of seawater, there were snowflakes caught in her eyelashes, and the island was shrouded in a thick, wet fog that made seeing anything almost impossible. But none of this was enough to stop the tremor of electricity that hummed through her veins. They had made it.

They were actually *in* the Arctic Circle.

It was as if she'd crossed some kind of invisible frontier on Earth. Compared to the parks, hedgerows, and fertile green countryside of back home, here the land was bare and barren, with occasional hints of dark gorse peeping up through the snow the only sign of wildlife. On the far side of the island, she could just about make out a trio of tall, steep granite mountains and skies that were like a ladder reaching right up into space.

But mostly, it was cold. The kind of cold that gets under your clothes, making you shiver from the inside out and long for a hot water bottle.

"Well?" Dad asked again.

April picked up the nearest crate, lifted her face to the sky, and stuck out her tongue to catch snowflakes. "Let's find out!"

With the help of a hand-pulled sledge, they spent the next couple of hours carting their belongings half a mile inland to their new home, which consisted of two wooden cabins. One for sleeping and a larger one where Dad could conduct his meteorological research.

They looked like all the other Norwegian houses she'd seen so far—pointed rooftops, painted wooden slats, and the whisper of a magical fairy tale about them. The only thing spoiling the scene was the squat generator perched nearby that was to provide their electricity.

The living cabin was all one level and had an exterior door opening onto a small porch where they could remove their coats, scarves, and the frosty, bitter outside air, and then an inner door that opened into an oblong-shaped room with a high arched ceiling, an open fireplace, and two worn sofas. In one corner of the room was a narrow bookshelf housing a handful of well-thumbed books and a satellite phone to be used in emergencies only. In the opposite corner was a kitchenette, leading into a dry storeroom with shelves crammed with canned food and enough provisions to last for six months.

Scattered around the main living area were remnants

of the former inhabitants. An ashtray with a cigarette stub. A solitary red glove. Some pieces of scrap paper and an old ballpoint pen.

But it was the map of the island tacked to the wall that *really* caught her eye. On a map of the world, Bear Island was nothing more than a pencil dot that sat somewhere between Norway and an archipelago of islands near the North Pole called Svalbard. (Although Bear Island was technically part of that archipelago, it was so far away, they were almost like two distinct places.) It was so tiny that, unless you knew it was there, you wouldn't even see it. April could relate to that. Most people tended to overlook her too.

Even though she knew the information already, she peered closer to read the dimensions. The island was actually about twelve miles long at its greatest north-to-south extension and roughly ten miles wide. While the northern part of the island was mountainous, the southern part consisted mostly of lowland plains

where a red cross marked the metrological station.
There was a treasure trove of coves, beaches, inland
lakes, and, of course, the trio of mountains she'd spotted from the beach—all to investigate and discover over
the next six months. Even if there *really* were no polar
bears, there would still be arctic foxes, thousands of
rare seabirds, and maybe even some migrating whales.
And perhaps the biggest bonus of all—spending time
with her father.

"Dad! Look at all the things we can do together!"
she said breathlessly. "Tomorrow, can we go to the
mountains and take the sled?"

She spun around thinking he was still in the room,
but there was nothing apart from the echo of her own
voice. Pushing down her disappointment, she peered
through the window and watched as he entered the
meteorological cabin and shut the door behind him.

April let out a deep sigh, and her warm breath
clouded the window. It was only day one, she told

herself sternly, and it was important he find his feet. There was really no need to be upset, because with six whole months ahead of them, they had the whole summer together yet. So she wiped the window clean, pulled back her shoulders, and decided to unpack instead.

An hour or so later, she was half dozing on the sofa and didn't hear Dad until he stood right in front her and cleared his throat with a gruff cough. She opened her eyes to find his thoughtful gaze upon her.

"Dad!"

He pushed a hand through his unruly hair, cleared his throat a couple more times, and then thrust a neatly wrapped gift into her hands.

This wasn't so much of a surprise, because he had a habit of giving gifts at unexpected moments. It almost, but not quite, made up for his absentmindedness around birthdays. She opened this one to reveal a slim silver watch the color of moonlight.

"I know . . . ," he said, chewing over his words carefully. "I know there is no one here but us and I appreciate this is an unusual turn of events and perhaps not one most people would approve of. Not your grandmother anyway."

April winced, remembering the tears at the airport.

"But," he continued, "there is a lot of wonder in a place like this. For centuries, people have been drawn to these parts of the world. Some come for science. Some come for discovery. Others come for reasons they don't even understand themselves." He swallowed a couple of times, suddenly looking as thin and fragile as one of his books. "Perhaps that is why I am here too—to find something I lost a long time ago."

When he managed to find his next words, his voice had a crack right down the middle. *"Frilufts-liv,"* he said while April gazed at him in confusion. "English is a very useful language but sometimes lacks the tools to describe certain experiences—or people.

It's a Norwegian word that means enjoyment of the outdoors. Literally, 'open-air life.'" His expression softened. "This word reminds me of you . . . the way you spend so much time in the yard. I look at you out of my study window sometimes and I . . . I swear I see your mother." April nodded, her breath held somewhere tight in her chest. She'd had no idea that Dad sometimes watched her, and the thought made her stomach cartwheel.

"She loved animals too, especially those in the wild. She had a rare affinity with them," said Dad. "She even said they could talk—but most humans had forgotten how to listen. That was your mother. She was . . . different from other people. Anyway, the point I'm trying to make is that she would have loved to come to somewhere like this. This watch was hers, and I thought, this way, at least she's experiencing it too."

"Friluftsliv," April repeated softly. It was a word that

sounded like mermaids, enchanted forests, or something ethereal and magic.

The memories April had of her mother were hazy. But one thing she did remember was how she would make hot chocolate in a bright red teapot, and then the three of them would perch on the edge of April's bed and drink it with cookies served on paper plates cut into daisies. Those were the days when the house was full of laughter, not sadness, and Dad would remember to kiss her good night. Instead of reading a bedtime story, they would take turns telling her about all the different animals in the world—the herds of elephants roaming across the plains of Africa, the rare Siberian tigers living in the mountains of Asia, the majestic emperor penguins who huddled up together to survive the long, bitter winters in the Antarctic, and some so strange and unusual—like the pangolin, whose entire body was made up of scales—it was hard to believe they weren't made up. Filled with the warm glow of her parents' voices, April would go to sleep with a smile on her face dreaming of Earth's many wonders.

These days, Dad rarely talked about her mother, let alone told bedtime stories, and so the gift of the watch felt like he'd tucked a warm, cozy hand around her heart.

"Friluftsliv," she said again, and found her throat had suddenly gotten thick.

It wasn't until a few moments later she thought to read the time.

It was eleven p.m.

She looked up, but Dad had already retreated to his bedroom, and she heard the slow waltz of a Mozart record start up. It was the one of the pieces played at their wedding, and she was never sure if it actually made him happier or not.

With nothing to do, she returned to her own

bedroom and flung open the window, where the cold, hard shock of the outside air made her lungs ache. Dad said the temperatures stayed very low even in the height of summer, and she felt glad they had brought so many clothes with them. Overhead, the fog had cleared to leave a dappled blue sky, and she squinted around her in surprise. Although the sun hung low in the sky, it was as bright outside as midday, with not a single sign of sunset. Even while the Mozart record played plaintively next door, a soft sigh of contentment escaped her lips. Despite the long day they'd had and all the travel they'd done, April didn't feel tired. Instead, her tummy bubbled with the kind of impatience you feel on Christmas Eve. What she really wanted was to get out there.

Her eyes traveled over the distant mountains, the wild seas to her left, and the flat, snow-covered land stretching out ahead. And then she did a double take. There on the horizon, silhouetted against the sun,

31

something moved. It was in the blink of an eye. So rapid she almost missed it. Something big and loping and most unexpected.

It couldn't be?

She blinked again. Whatever it was had gone.

But April could have sworn she'd just seen a polar bear.

EXPLORATION

"I'M GOING EXPLORING," April announced. As it was their first full day, she had waited most of the morning for Dad to suggest a walk or some kind of adventure. But come lunchtime, she'd had enough of twiddling her thumbs. She pulled on her boots, red hat, and mittens, and glanced his way purposefully.

"Hmmmm?" He was engrossed in the paperwork his predecessor had left and failed to feel the weight of her stare. "I need to get started on the temperatures. You go without me." Surrounded by important-looking logbooks, he wafted a hand in her direction, which showed he didn't really mind what she did as long as she didn't bother him.

"Are you sure you don't want to come?" She pressed her nose up against the window. "It looks so . . . perfect out there."

"Another day, April," he replied without even looking up. "Perhaps when I'm not so busy. There's a lot more work here than I'd anticipated."

With a reluctant backward glance, she headed outside. The sun hung bright in the sky and glinted off the snow like stardust, but the shock of the cold still surprised her. It crept down the side of her rain jacket and then crawled across her skin and seeped into her bones. But despite the cold, or maybe because of it, the air felt clean. It was a smell that reminded her of freshly washed sheets or the way the seaside smelled after a storm.

It smelled so good, she wanted to drink it.

With a deep inhale, she set off in the general

direction of where she thought she'd seen the polar bear. Common sense told her it was probably nothing more than a trick of the peculiar light that seemed to exist in this part of the world. But it didn't stop her from checking it out.

The thought of sharing a deserted island with a polar bear might have scared some children—but not April. It didn't even cross her mind to be afraid. In fact, she felt the opposite—a shimmery glimmer of excitement, as if someone had sprinkled glitter all over her. Here was the wide world her mother had always talked about, and April was actually living right inside it.

But after about an hour's walking, she was out of breath and her hopes were fizzling. Even though the terrain was flat, more than once she'd stepped into an unexpectedly deep pocket of snow and left one of her boots behind. Even though she was wearing her thermals, a thin cotton sweater, a fleece, and blue waterproof trousers (regulation pairs that were assigned to both her and her father), she still wore her own red waterproof jacket on top and a brand-new pair of rainbow boots. Despite all of this, her socks were damp, her nose was red, and her eyes were runny from the wind.

"Hello!" she cried, her voice sounding odd and tinny in all the emptiness. "Is anybody here?!"

She cocked her ear and listened but heard nothing apart from the soft sound of falling snow and the distant roar of the sea.

It was completely unlike home—the constant hum of traffic, the overhead grumble of planes, the choke and smell of engines, the millions of people on the streets scurrying and hurrying to get somewhere. It was not even like Granny Apples's farm, which was full of ripe apple trees rustling in the breeze, the smell of baking, and the distant shouts of children playing in the turquoise bay.

Everything here was quiet. Untouched. Like a photograph she had inadvertently stepped into. Apart from the gulls—and many other seabirds she didn't recognize—the only evidence of life was her footprints in the snow. She gazed at them, spiraling behind her like a trail of bread crumbs. It was an empty place. A place that could be very lonely if you had no one to share it with. Perhaps this was the thing Tör had warned her about. This feeling of being on the edge of the Earth. The sense that if she looked up, she would be able to look from this world into the next one.

She kept walking for two more hours, until it was simply too cold to walk anymore and her nose felt like it was about to drop off. All the time she had kept her eyes peeled for any proof of the polar bear—searching for evidence like polar bear poop, killed seals, or paw prints—looking for something to make sense of what she had seen last night.

But she didn't spot a single sign of them.

★

"Why is it called Bear Island?" she asked over dinner that evening. She had come home and spent the rest of the day in front of the fire warming up. "If there are no polar bears here?"

Dad had finally put his logbooks down, and they sat side by side on the sofa eating their dinner straight from the can. It was only day one, but by unspoken agreement, they had decided that plates and bowls were an unnecessary addition to mealtimes.

He put his beef stew on the floor and adjusted his position so he faced her. "Because once upon a time the island was full of bears."

"So it really *is* called Bear Island because of the bears?" April asked, delighted to have his full attention. "I thought maybe it was just a made-up name."

"No. It's real," Dad said, looking pleased to be able to share some of his knowledge. "It dates back to 1596, when the first recorded killing of a polar bear took place on this island. They fought with the bear for over two hours before eventually killing it—then afterward they called the island Bear Island."

"*Two* hours?" she said with an ache to her heart. "The poor thing."

"It was just what they did back in those days."

April frowned. "So there are no bears because people *killed* them all?"

"That," he said, "and the ice caps."

April knew that ice caps formed in winter and then melted in summer and looked a bit like interlinked jigsaw pieces floating on the water. She also knew that once upon a time there were way more ice caps than there were now. But what she didn't know was how this affected Bear Island.

"The ice caps used to extend this far south," Dad explained.

"Which meant that the bears could reach the island in winter?"

"Exactly," he replied. "Polar bears are mostly marine animals, and they use the ice caps as hunting ground to catch seals. But since the ice caps have been melting, it means they can't travel as far as they used to. That's why the polar bear population is dropping. Not just here—but all across the Arctic."

April sat thinking over her can of chickpea stew. (She had been a proud vegetarian for over two years.) "But if the ice caps around here are melting . . ."

"Melted," Dad corrected.

"Melted," April amended. "If the ice caps around here have melted, does that mean a bear can *never* get back to Bear Island?"

"Not if there aren't any ice caps. The nearest polar bear population is based in Svalbard, which is nearly two hundred and fifty miles away. In the old days, that's where they would have traveled from to get to

Bear Island, but now it's just too far for them to swim."

"Not even one?" she asked in a tiny voice, picturing the bear in her mind.

"Not even one."

5

WALRUS BAY

IN THE COUPLE OF WEEKS that followed, the pair of them settled into a rhythm. It wasn't a rhythm April had expected or even wanted, but it was, at least, familiar. Dad would get up first thing and disappear to work, although on Bear Island, work wasn't a commute across a busy city but instead just a short thirty-second walk into the meteorological cabin. However, because measuring the temperatures was pretty much an all-day job, he didn't reappear until well past dinnertime.

April kept a spark of hope alive that he might one day announce they would go sledding, or make a snowman, or even just take a walk together, but with each passing day, that spark grew dimmer and dimmer. More than once she'd overheard him muttering about the amount of work he was expected to do. At times of stress, he could be prone to temper outbursts. They were never long or ill meant, but they had the force of a flash storm and so April watched warily from the sidelines in case one was accidentally directed her way. After one particularly long, tense day, she even offered to help him with his temperatures, but he'd barked that it wasn't work for little girls. All of which meant she had a lot of spare time on her hands—way more than she'd wanted to have, anyway.

Her day looked a bit like this:

6 a.m.–7 a.m.—Lie in bed and count down the seconds until she had to get up. Even though it was mid-April, it was still bitterly cold all day in the Arctic Circle but much worse first thing, especially when you had forgotten to bring your slippers with you.

7 a.m.—Breakfast. Normally dry oat biscuits, which weren't so bad when you slathered them with peanut butter. (April had brought a lot of jars of peanut butter with her.) But on Sundays, they had what they wanted, and she normally chose chocolate cookies with a giant mug of hot chocolate.

8 a.m.–12 a.m.—School, but only Monday to Friday.

It wasn't a real school, of course. How could it be? But, because Dad had promised April's teacher that he would homeschool her, he'd brought with him six encyclopedias—one for each month she was here. It probably wasn't what the teachers had in mind. But even though the writing was tiny and the pages smelled of dust, they had beautiful pictures of animals inside and, more important, taught her about the part of the world she now found herself in.

In this way, she learned how the word *arctic* came from the Greek word *arktos*, which meant "bear." She also found out the Arctic Circle wasn't a real circle at all but more of an invisible line that girded the top part of the Earth, encompassing many different countries, including Norway, Russia, Finland, Canada, and America. And how, out of the *entire* world's population, only four million people actually lived within that circle all year round—people like Tör and his father. Moments like these, she wished she could speak to Tör and ask him the kind of questions the encyclopedias didn't have space to answer. But even though he'd given her his number, she suspected the satellite phone wasn't for conversations such as whether the Sami really had 180 different words for snow.

12 p.m.—Lunch. April usually heated up a can of tomato soup and ate it with some more oat biscuits. She would take Dad's soup into the weather cabin—as she had taken to calling it—and leave it on the side for him so as not to disturb him.

12:30–late—Polar bear hunting.

Because, regardless of what Dad said, she wasn't prepared to admit there was no bear here. Besides, with him being so busy, it gave April something to do. And so, armed with a pair of binoculars, a compass, her rainbow boots, her hat, mittens, and about a thousand layers, she set off every afternoon to look for him.

As the days passed, the ground snow slowly started to thaw, and before long, it was no longer possible to retrace her footprints. Luckily, Dad had shown her how to use the compass and explained how, if she set it to south, she would always find her way back to the cabins. The only word of caution he gave her was to not venture too close to the sea's edge—lest a freak wave sweep her away. The water in the Arctic was freezing and would kill her in just a handful of minutes.

Other than that, she had free rein and could do what she wanted.

Of course, she kept her mission a secret. She knew he would tell her that polar bears were highly dangerous and would most likely love to eat a girl like her. But it didn't stop her from looking.

"Where are you?" she called out. "Where are you hiding?"

It took nearly another whole week of searching.

In that time, she also reluctantly adjusted to the truth that, while she and Dad were the only two humans on the island, she might as well be here alone for all the time he spent with her. Despite that, Bear Island was finally starting to feel like home—albeit an out-of-the-ordinary one. The island had a mysterious current all of its own, and without her even being aware of it, the sounds and echoes and noise of her old city life faded away. The tall and dark house became blurred around the edges and hard to remember. Even Granny Apples's home by the sea started to lose color. And school was something she completely forgot— although, admittedly, that wasn't hard to do. It was like being in a whole new world. And the closest to living in a magical story that April had ever felt.

With the snow melting more and more each day, she'd discovered inland lakes, some so blue they matched the color of the sea. She'd leaped over gurgling streams furrowing their way down from the snowcapped mountains toward the sea. She'd lain on her back and watched thousands of gulls sweeping overhead in a majestic white arc. Once, she'd even seen a solitary arctic fox, still and poised in the distance, his fur a shimmering velvety white. April had held her breath in wonder as the spell of the island wrapped its hold around her.

All she needed now was to find her polar bear.

"You are a him, aren't you?" she said out loud. "I know you're a boy. I don't know how I know. But I do."

Sometimes she had the feeling that he was out there watching her. It wasn't a concrete feeling—but a sixth sense. A sensation of not always being alone. But whenever she snapped her head up and gazed around, there was nothing to see apart from sunlight, mountains, or crashing waves.

★

She'd already explored about half the island, and this afternoon, she planned to visit an old whaling station in a cove called Walrus Bay on the far side. Years and years ago, it was a place where humans had tried to live but failed. To get there, she passed a handful of the shimmery inland lakes and headed toward the trio of mountains.

Although Walrus Bay didn't look far on the map, getting there took a lot longer than April thought it would, and after nearly three hours, she was almost ready to turn back. Although the sun stayed in the sky until nearly midnight, she didn't like being out too late. There was a strange fog that often settled on the island in the late afternoon, clinging to it like a ghost and making the light take on an eerie yellow hue.

It was then she heard the noise.

April cocked her head. It was not a noise she'd heard before, either on Bear Island or back home. It was not even a human noise. It reminded her of something, but no matter how hard she dug, she couldn't find the memory. She stood absolutely still, her breath unfurling in the cold air like smoke. The noise stopped, and she let out a deep, relieved sigh. It wasn't the kind of noise you would want to listen to for long. It was deep and guttural and made her skin tighten. But just as quickly as she thought it was gone, it started again. Louder this time.

April realized what it reminded her of: the time three years ago when one of the foxes had gotten its paw trapped in a rusted tin can and couldn't get it off. The horrible gut-wrenching sound of an animal in pain.

"Oh no." April's heart squeezed tight. There was no way she could turn back now. Not when there was an animal who might need her help. Not when there was no one else to save them but her. She half ran, stumbled, and skidded the last remaining few hundred yards, her breath aching in her throat and her chest burning until she finally arrived at Walrus Bay.

And then she shuddered to a halt.

The fog was already starting to creep in, slowly slithering along the ground. There was a jetty jutting into the bay, but so long disused that it was now just a series of loose rotting slats. Elsewhere, there was a wooden hut with the door hanging off its hinges and the windows long since broken. Upturned on the shore was the abandoned hull of an old fishing boat. A rusting pile of cable sat next to it. Partly shrouded in the creepy fog, the whole scene looked like something out of a ghost movie.

And then the noise came again.

Much closer now. This time so fierce and loud and frightening, it sent a shiver down her spine. Even if she'd wanted to run away, she couldn't. Instead, she became rooted to the ground as every nerve in her body buzzed and hummed like electricity. It was as if time suddenly froze, or at least slowed down. The air itself felt sharp and still. The wind stopped. Even the sea held its breath.

And April knew that if she looked up, her life would never be the same again. That this moment itself was going to alter her in some way. Maybe even forever.

She slowly raised her eyes.

And there, standing on the other side of the beach, about 150 feet away, was the most magnificent creature she had ever seen.

6

HURT

HE STOOD ON HIS two hind legs, rearing up like a brilliant white stallion into the sky. With his chin jutted forward confidently, he didn't look in pain. In fact, he stood in a way that indicated he knew just how magnificent he was.

The combination of powerful muscle and raw brute strength took April's breath clean away, and she clapped her hands over her mouth to stop herself from gasping out loud.

"You're the most incredible thing I've ever seen," she whispered, and without her even knowing why, a tear trickled down her face. Not because she was sad.

But because it was the only way for the size of the emotion to come out. The way sometimes watching the news about the destruction of the Amazon made her scream in anger, or how some books made her want to break out in a silly song when they got to the mushy part, or even how one or two pieces of Dad's music stirred and twisted her emotions so much, the only way they could come out was by dancing.

The feelings swung from awe to wonder to joy and then mixed together like a milkshake, so she felt dizzy and light-headed with them. Tör had been wrong, she thought with a smile, and for a brief moment, she wished he were here with her so he could see the bear with his own eyes.

"I knew I wasn't imagining things," she said, at last finding her voice. "I did see you that night. You *are* real."

Even from this distance, the bear pricked up his ears as if he could hear her. She supposed his sense of hearing was better than hers, given that his ears were a lot larger. He sniffed the air, his black nose twitching against the cold and the damp fog. And then, ever so slowly, he turned around, and across the beach they locked eyes.

April remembered she had the binoculars slung over her shoulder, and so, hurriedly with cold, clammy fingers, she slipped them out of their cover and planted them against her face. At first, she could see nothing but a blurry smudge. So she twisted and turned the little thumb wheel until he gradually came into sharp, defined focus.

"Why, you're beautiful," she breathed out. "You're the most beautiful thing I've ever seen. Look at you! You're like . . ." She reached for a word to try to describe him but could only come up with a particular piece of music Dad loved to listen to that made April think of erupting volcanoes, violent storms, and huge tidal waves. "You're like that," she decided.

At which point, the bear's mouth opened into the hugest, biggest, most cavernous roar, and even from this distance, April could feel the power of it, the way sound travels invisibly through the air and shifts the membrane of the universe somehow. Such a deafening, earsplitting roar made her teeth chatter, and she dropped the binoculars on her feet.

He might be beautiful, but even from this distance, he was also terrifying. The sheer raw power of him made her breath squeeze against her ribs.

The bear dropped to all fours and lurched forward, taking a step toward her. April let out an involuntary whimper. A burned feeling scorched through her nerve endings, and her breathing was tight and shallow, trapped somewhere in her throat. What if he came closer? What if he attacked? But just as quickly as he'd moved, the bear stopped abruptly. There was something cautious about the way he was keeping to the other side of the beach. Of course, he would be just as wary of her as she was of him, and she let out a deep, shaky breath of relief.

Picking up the binoculars once more, she chewed her lip in worry, because he really was desperately thin. She could even see his ribs poking through his fur. And surely his fur should look shinier and far less matted than that.

There was also a sharpness to his face. Not a horrible sharpness the way some people's faces are sharp permanently. But a sharpness born of hunger and desperation.

"Oh, you poor thing," she murmured. "You're starving."

He inclined his head, so slightly that April almost missed it.

"Are you hungry?" she asked. "You're not going to eat me, are you?"

She scanned the rest of his face quickly through the binoculars. Even though he was a wild animal, he did look friendly—for a polar bear, anyway. The tickly whiskers, the soft, wet black of his nose, and his dark, chocolate-colored eyes, which, even from this distance, seemed gentle.

She cleared her throat and wondered what to say next.

"My name is April," she offered at last. "April Wood. I'm eleven years old, I like hot chocolate, especially with marshmallows on top, and I'm here with my dad, who's measuring the temperatures for six months. He said there were no bears left on the island, but I *knew* I'd seen you that first night. Why would you risk coming so close to the cabin? Maybe . . ." She stopped as the idea hit her. "Maybe you *wanted* to be seen? But why would that be?"

She gazed at him in puzzlement, and it wasn't until she scanned her binoculars over his whole body that she finally saw it.

"Oh my!" she exclaimed in horror. "What have you done to yourself?"

His front left paw had something tightly wrapped around it—a blue plastic of some kind. He brought the paw up to his mouth and gnawed at it with long, sharp teeth, growling under his breath as he tried to bite it off. But it was no use. The paw had swollen to twice its size, and the plastic had wound its way impossibly tight—there was no way it was coming off. His head remained hung low, and he looked so vulnerable, pathetic even, that April's first instinct was to run across and give him a big squeezy hug even though she knew how dangerous that would be.

"That looks so painful," April murmured. She wanted to help, but there was a big difference between letting a seagull sit on your hand and approaching a wild polar bear. She swallowed hard. "What about if I search for something sharp so you can cut yourself free?"

She wasn't sure of the wisdom of her plan, but since it was better than doing nothing, she rummaged on the beach, trying to find something, *anything*, that would help him. She did find a bit of glass, green like a mermaid's tale, but it had long since been smoothed by the sea. There were other bits of debris that had been washed ashore from lands and seas far away. Some tangled fishing net, driftwood, plastic water bottles even—which made April growl herself. There were other things she couldn't even recognize. But what she didn't find was anything sharp. Anyway, what good would it have done? It wasn't like he could cut himself free, otherwise he would have done that by now already.

"It's no use," she said eventually, the frustration in her voice echoing forlornly across the windswept bay. She felt the bear's gaze rest upon her, and April didn't think she'd ever felt as small or useless as she did in that moment.

But what could she do? The sun had dropped lower in the sky. It was late. Too late for her to be out alone.

"I'm so sorry, but I have to go now." She looked at the sun once more, now so low it was almost touching the surface of the sea, and then turned her gaze back to the bear. His head had sunk dejectedly onto his paws, and his whole body radiated sadness. April's heart lurched. "I'll be back," she whispered. "I promise."

And the bear lifted up his head and roared.

APRIL'S DECISION

HOW HAD THE BEAR ended up on the island, exactly how long had he been here, and how come none of the previous meteorologists had seen him before now? The answers sat annoyingly out of reach, and April banged the saucepan down in frustration. It was dinnertime, and she couldn't help but think of how hungry the poor bear had looked. His damaged paw must have been stopping him from hunting properly. What would he be eating tonight? And what could *she* do to help?

As she racked her brains, Dad wandered into the living room, yawned loudly, and emptied his pockets onto the table. Amid some aniseed candy wrappers, a chewed pen, and a hankie, his Swiss Army knife clattered onto the hard surface. She didn't know why he carried it around, because he only ever used it for cutting his toenails.

She was about to empty the beans into the saucepan, and then her hand froze.

The knife.

What if she tried to cut the plastic off herself?

She waited until Dad had disappeared to take his final readings of the day before picking it up and holding it tentatively in her hands. She'd never really used a knife before, except for cutting apples and carrots and things like that, but . . .

Her thoughts trailed off. Because the truth was, even though she had used a knife before, she had never used one on a polar bear. Never on an animal that might actually *kill* her.

★

She barely slept that night, as her mind kept returning to Tör's warning on the boat. He was right. The animals here were nothing like back home. They had been born in complete wilderness with zero contact with humans. Even an arctic fox was completely different from the foxes in their backyard. This part of the world was far more dangerous.

She tossed and turned, pulled this way and that by the currents in her heart. However, when she woke up in the morning, she swung her legs out of bed, took a deep breath, and squared her shoulders.

Deep down, when she thought about it, there was only one choice. She would take Dad's knife and cut the bear free.

Because if she didn't do it, who would?

Come lunch, she quickly heated a can of minestrone soup for Dad and carried it over to the weather cabin.

"Oh . . . thanks, April." Dad looked up distractedly. "Is it lunch already?"

She nodded. "I brought you these as well." She dropped a handful of aniseed candies on the counter. Dad had brought enough to last exactly six months and rationed himself to three a day.

While he busied himself unwrapping a candy as a starter, April seized the Swiss Army knife from his jacket pocket and quickly sidled out the door. She then pulled on her coat and boots, grabbed some oat biscuits and a jar of peanut butter from the storeroom, and set off.

The walk to Walrus Bay didn't feel as long today, partly because she knew exactly where she was heading and what she was doing—even if the prospect was already making her mouth dry. She took a deep breath for bravery, and around her, the air felt sharp and clean, as if the Earth were made of crunchy edible crystals. In fact, it almost felt as though the island knew her mission and was on her side.

"Nearly there," she murmured, and just minutes later, she arrived with a self-conscious laugh of relief because in the crisp, clear light of day, Walrus Bay didn't seem half as spooky as yesterday, when everything, including Bear, had initially felt so big and alarming.

The only trouble was there was no sign of him, even when she gazed through her binoculars at every conceivable point on the horizon—the trio of snow-capped mountains, the barren flat land where she'd just walked from, and the ramshackle ruins that tumbled onto the beach. She next scanned the binoculars over the plunging gray surf. Bears could swim very well. Better than her, anyway—she much preferred climbing trees. But he didn't emerge from the sea, and because she had started to shiver and it was really no fun just waiting around, April decided to make herself useful.

She often picked up litter on the beaches near Granny Apples's house, so out of force of habit, April scoured the beach for anything that didn't belong there, and by the end she had accumulated twenty-six plastic bottles for various soft drinks. Seven rusting cans. A black comb. A pink unicorn toothbrush. A large pile of blue netting presumably used for fishing. A random toy car. And one half-full whiskey bottle. All brought to the island by the capricious currents of the sea from people far, far away.

"That's it." She placed the last bottle on the neat pile she had made by the upturned boat. Another day, she would come back with a bag and collect it all up.

But good deeds aside, she was starving, and there was still no sign of the polar bear. Even though she'd brought the oat biscuits as a gift, she suddenly felt ravenous—no wonder, because she'd forgotten to make any soup for herself. So she sat with her back to the hull, smothered the biscuits with peanut butter, and took a hungry mouthful. It was only when she looked up, crumbs on her chin and her mouth all sticky, that she realized she wasn't alone.

Not ten feet away stood the polar bear.

"Oh!" April said, so shocked that she dropped the jar of peanut butter and a big splotch of it splattered onto her right boot. "Where did you come from?"

Even though he was heartbreakingly skinny, up close he was still much huger than any animal she had ever seen before. April was perhaps about a third of his size, if that, and her neck crooked as she gazed up at him.

She spoke fast so she wouldn't lose her courage. "I've come to help you. See, I brought Dad's knife. I've never really used it before, but I'm sure it'll be okay. I just have to figure out which blade to use—there's so many! There's even a corkscrew—not that Dad drinks, because he doesn't. Not since the car accident. *He* was drinking. The boy, I mean. Not Dad. That's why he didn't see Mom. Not until it was too late. Dad hates drinking."

She was jabbering but, for some reason, couldn't seem to stop. "Anyway, you don't want to hear about that. I've just cleaned the beach. Can you see? That litter didn't belong here. Not on Bear Island. But I suppose people don't even know that places like this exist. I didn't. Not in real life anyway. I mean, I knew they existed in stories, but that's not the same thing is it? I didn't know Earth could look like *this*."

She swept her hand to indicate, what? The wildness? The emptiness? The feeling she wasn't even on Earth at all but had somehow stumbled onto a coarser, more desolate sister planet. Her hands dropped to her side, and she swallowed hard.

Nerves, she concluded. Not surprising, given the fact a human-eating polar bear was standing in front of her. She didn't dare look up. Even from ten feet away, she could feel his breath on her face, and it wasn't particularly pleasant. Her tummy squiggled and lurched, and for a horrible moment, she thought she was going to be sick.

"Come on, April," she whispered to herself. "Pull yourself together." Then she squared her shoulders, took a deep breath, and looked up, directly at him.

BEAR

"HELLO," APRIL SAID, making absolutely sure to keep as still as possible. She knew from her experience with the foxes in her yard that the worst thing to do would be to try to reach out. Animals had to come to you, not the other way around. If you rushed them, they either ran off, bit you, or—in this case—ate you alive.

She supposed it must be the same thing with polar bears. It was all about trust, no matter what size the animal. With that, April crossed her fingers and prepared to wait. All day if necessary. But hopefully not all night because Dad would worry then.

"You know my name, so I feel like I need to know

your name now," she said in a gentle voice. She had a soft voice most of the time—she had long learned that animals didn't like shouty, braying humans. And out here in the wilderness, she tried to make her voice sound softer than ever, like snowflakes. "But at the same time, it doesn't feel right to give you a name, like I would a cat or a dog. You're not even like Braveheart, because he lived in our backyard in the middle of the city. You're *completely* wild. And wild animals don't need human names. But I have to call you something, so I'm just going to call you Bear."

Bear didn't show any reaction, but she liked to think he approved.

"You like it, then, Bear?" she said. "You like your new name?"

She could have sworn his chocolate eyes crinkled around the edges, and April smiled. "I'll take that as a yes.

"Of course, I know you can't really speak to me,"

she went on. "But there has to be some kind of interpretation between us. It's like being a code breaker—I just need to decipher the signs."

She waited expectantly for some kind of affirmation. Anything would do—a nose waggle or an ear twitch. But after she'd spent several long seconds gazing at him intently, nothing appeared forthcoming.

"It doesn't matter," she said. "I know you're listening anyway. We can still communicate. People say animals can't speak, but I know that's not true. What was it my mom said? We just have to find a different way of talking, that's all." April glanced instinctively at her watch, as if half expecting her mother to materialize out of it like a genie.

Bear's ears twitched, but he still didn't come any closer. "You don't need to be scared of me. I'm not like grown-ups—I'm not going to hurt you," she said while swallowing down her own fear. "I just want to help."

However, no matter how much she reassured him in her most gentle of voices, Bear didn't venture any closer, and since April was still cautious about approaching him, they stayed in this unproductive impasse for the better part of two hours.

Until suddenly she had an idea.

"Now then, Bear—I've brought you some oat biscuits, and I'm not really *that* hungry. So I'm going to put some peanut butter on one—like this—and I'm going to leave it in front of me. Just there. On that little rock. Can you see? And if you want it, you are very welcome to it."

At first, Bear didn't react. Maybe he didn't like peanut butter as much as she did? Then he stuck his nose into the air, and it started to quiver and tremble. He took a couple of loud sniffs, and April could have sworn his eyes lit up just a little bit.

"It's peanut butter," she said. "Crunchy, because

that's the best kind. You'll like it. It's not seal or anything, but it's really very nice, especially if you're hungry."

Bear sniffed again, and his face was full of such a keen yearning that his whole body trembled this time. Very slowly, he took one tentative step forward, then another, until finally he took the third and last step, and without once taking his black eyes off April, he gobbled the oat biscuit all up.

"I knew you would like it!"

She was still smiling to herself when suddenly Bear lunged openmouthed directly toward her with his sharp pointed teeth. Death stared her in the face, and April wished she had said goodbye to Dad before leaving today. She clamped her eyes shut, crossed her fingers, and prayed there would be something left of her to bury.

Yet rather than get her head bitten off, April suddenly felt her right foot vibrating—as if something or someone was rubbing it strenuously, like some kind of deep tissue massage. She squeezed open one eye and peeped down. Where she'd dropped it earlier, Bear was licking the remains of the peanut butter off her boot with a gigantic pink tongue. It was like being licked by a cat—but a million times more powerful.

"Bear!" she squeaked. "There's nothing left!"

He took one last satisfying lick, then sat back on his haunches and gazed straight at her. His teeth were still bared, but as he was licking his lips and sweeping his tongue all over his jaw, he didn't look half as imposing as before.

"You want more, do you?"

She gingerly placed the last remaining oat biscuits on the rock and watched as he gobbled them up in less than a second. When he finished, he tilted his head to the left and looked at her pleadingly.

"There's none left!" she said. "I'm sorry."

His ears drooped, and April wished she'd brought

another pack, especially now that he had backed off again and stood watching her from a cautious distance. Despite the knife sitting in her pocket and the swollen paw, which was obviously causing great pain, April realized she wouldn't be able to get near him again. Not unless she had more food anyway.

"I'll come back tomorrow," she said, not quite sure if she felt relieved or disappointed.

The next day, she brought ten packs of oat biscuits and two jars of peanut butter, and this time, it only took an hour before Bear tentatively approached and ate the food she'd laid out for him at a safe distance. The day after that, it had reduced to half an hour. And the day after that, it took just ten minutes before he felt trusting enough. By now, she was also feeling slightly calmer around him. He hadn't shown any sign of wanting to eat her—only the food she brought. And so, when she arrived on the fifth day after first meeting him, this time it was as if Bear were waiting for her, and he hobbled straight up to her.

She placed the food and backed up about ten paces and took a deep steadying breath. Then, without pausing, lest fear get in the way, she curled her fingers around the knife in her pocket.

"Now, are you going to let me look at your paw?"

FRIENDSHIP

IT WAS A HUGE PAW; polar bears' paws had to be big to spread the bear's weight over the ice, but it was even huger with the swelling. A piece of plastic, the kind you find around a six-pack of cans—but obviously of a more industrial scale—had gotten caught around his paw. Tied in with that was some blue fishing net. They had gotten so scrambled up, there was no way he could get it off himself.

She swallowed down any last bits of fear and made herself stand absolutely still. Not like a statue but a soft kind of stillness—like water, just like how she had instructed Tör. She breathed deep and slow, all the way down to her belly, and her breath was almost silent, the only evidence the cloudy droplets in the cold air. From the soles of her boots, she imagined roots connecting her to the island, the way the island sometimes seemed to want to reach up and connect with her. In this way, she became less human somehow and more bear.

"May I touch it?" she asked gently, because there was no way she was foolish enough to touch a wild animal without permission.

Bear had eaten all the food but not moved away. Did he know she wanted to help him? Or had she just reached a level of trust with him that he felt safer around her? Either way, she kept her eyes pinned to his face. He gazed at her so long and unblinkingly, she wasn't sure how much time passed. The outside world had shrunk to the space between them and the slow, steady intermingling of their breath.

Knowing the right moment to move wasn't based

on logic. This wasn't a game of chess. It was instinct. Something she didn't even have to question or doubt. And in that way, she finally allowed herself to take a tiny step toward him.

"See," she said. "I'm not going to hurt you."

She paused before cautiously taking the next step, before pausing again and then taking the next. Each step brought her closer and closer, until she was just one small step away. So close she could count the outlines of each of his long black whiskers and feel the wetness of his nose.

Her fingers tightened around the knife, and breathing calmly, she slowly brought it out of her pocket and held it in front of her face. Bear blinked but didn't back away.

"I'm going to use this to cut off the plastic," she said. "But you have to promise you won't hurt me."

By this point she was so close, she could stare straight into his eyes. They were the color of deep rich chocolate, so brown they appeared almost black. There was a story in his eyes, as there is with every person and animal. And Bear's eyes spoke of hunger and desperation. Perhaps loneliness too, although April wasn't sure if that was a reflection of her own feelings or not. But, most important, they weren't unkind or cruel like some eyes are, and as she searched deep within them, she finally got the permission she needed.

With a deep, steadying breath, she crouched down, took off her mitten, and then reached out her hand. She could feel his breath on the back of her neck and sense his teeth poised above her like a guillotine. And then her fingers tentatively touched his fur. "Oh! You're so soft!" His fur was like a warm, cozy blanket but smelled of seawater and wilderness. The plastic had dug so deep, she couldn't even get her fingers under it. As she touched the area where it cut in, Bear trembled.

"Oh, you poor thing," she said. "Let me try to cut it off."

Even with the knife, it took a full ten minutes before she managed to snip away all the fishing net and then cut through the plastic. The whole time, she had to be so careful she wasn't cutting into his skin—she didn't think she blinked through the whole operation—but finally his paw was free.

When the last bit of plastic dropped to the ground, Bear lifted up his head and roared. It was so earsplitting, April actually fell to the beach facedown. Even then, he continued to roar, making the earth tremble and the heavens roll and the skies splinter.

"That's quite all right," said April, lifting herself up once he had finished. "I know you're just saying thank you."

Bear looked at her with his dark brown eyes, twinkling not just with the reflection of the sea but with something far deeper. It was a look that covered time and space and everything in between. And it could have lasted forever or it could have lasted seconds.

Looking back, she was never quite sure.

But one thing she did know: it was the kind of look that friendships could be forged upon.

"I'll come back tomorrow," she said somewhat shakily as she got to her feet and tried to make sense of a new version of life where a girl like her could potentially be friends with a polar bear. "I'll bring some antiseptic ointment to put on your paw to stop any infection."

Bear opened his mouth to roar, but this time she held up her hand to stop him midflow. "And yes," she said, giggling. "Some peanut butter too."

THE MIDNIGHT SUN

APRIL SKIPPED AND HOPPED and danced the whole way home. Her insides tingled, and her heart shone. She would come back tomorrow—bring some more peanut butter. Maybe a whole jar this time and some oat biscuits. Perhaps two packs. What else did polar bears eat apart from seal? She would find out!

So it was that she tumbled through the cabin door in a kaleidoscope of ideas, excitement, and breathlessness, like a carnival blazing with color and noise and cotton candy. Her cheeks glowing not just with the cold but with a kind of happiness she hadn't felt for a long time.

And then she stopped dead in her tracks.

Dad was sitting cross-legged in front of the fire smiling at her. Actually, *really* smiling, not the mouth-only one he'd worn since arriving.

"Dad?" she asked tentatively. "Is everything okay?"

He didn't answer right away. Instead, he sprang to his feet and put on his favorite Mozart tune. It was the fun one—Sonata no. 17—the one that made her want to twirl around the room in a goofy waltz. "It's tonight!" he said as the music leaped and bubbled around them.

"What's tonight?"

"The midnight sun, April. The midnight sun!"

The midnight sun was something Dad had talked about before they came. It had, in fact, been part of his sales pitch to Granny Apples—that everyone should witness the midnight sun at least once in their lives. And April, lucky April, was going to get nearly a whole summer of it. His pitch had fallen flat because

Granny Apples grumbled that, even though their own sun was weak and unreliable, it was still good enough for her.

But then, it's always hard to imagine things you've never seen before. Now, with the music dancing around the room, the bouncy waltz in her step, and Dad's grin of excitement, April felt a buzz of lightning run through her.

She, April Wood, had not only helped a polar bear today, but she was also about to see the midnight sun!

Of course, they had to wait until midnight, and that was still four hours away; but in the meantime, she heated two cans of vegetable soup, and they sat slurping it side by side on the sofa, resting the tins on two of the dusty old encyclopedias.

"Tell me about the midnight sun," she ventured, sensing Dad was in the mood to talk.

She was right. He took the empty cans, placed them

on the floor, and sank into the sofa with a relaxed grunt of satisfaction. "You remember that globe I bought you for your birthday a few years back?"

April nodded. It'd actually been two days after her birthday and she'd really wanted a kitten, but the globe turned out to be a nice present.

"Then you know that we are near the North Pole. Not *at* the North Pole but somewhere close. And you'll also know that the Earth sits on an axis." He demonstrated with his coffee cup by tilting it a few degrees to the right. "And because this axial tilt of the Earth is so great, this means that in summer the sun does not set in the parts of the world that are closer to the poles—like here." He pointed to the top and bottom of the mug. "Depending on how close to the pole you are, the sun can stay out for months without even setting once. Some people refer to it as the polar day. But it is more commonly known as the midnight sun."

"You mean it doesn't get dark at *all*?"

"That's correct," he answered. "There is no night."

April tried to wrap her head around a day with no night. She'd noticed how the nights had been getting lighter and lighter, but the sun had always dipped below the horizon. Now the sun would stay in the sky the *entire* time. One thing puzzled her. "But how do people sleep?"

Dad turned to her and grinned. "By closing their eyes of course."

It wasn't even funny—Dad's jokes tended not to be—but because she couldn't even *remember* the last time he'd made a joke, April found herself gurgling with laughter anyway and then Dad joined in and the pair of them laughed till their sides ached.

When the laughter died down, April scrambled her brains for another question. It was not often she had this kind of moment with her father, so she wanted to stretch it out and make it last as long as possible. "And you get the opposite too, don't you?"

"Yes," he said, looking pleased to be asked. "Come Christmastime, the sun does not even rise at all in these parts of the world. Imagine that? A winter of complete darkness. But we don't have to worry about that, as we shall be gone long before then."

They had been here just over one month already, which meant five months to go. Five whole months of summer. It didn't even matter so much anymore that Dad had to work so hard, because she was filled with excitement about getting to know Bear better. With no nights, it almost felt as though she'd been gifted double the number of days to spend with him.

A little before midnight, and dressed head to toe in jackets, boots, hats, scarves, and gloves, they stepped outside into the cold. The first thing April did was look up. It was true. The sky wasn't a soft velvety black.

There were no twinkling stars. She couldn't even see a moon. Instead, the sun hung low on the horizon, and the sky around it was streaked with orange.

April gazed at it in wonder as her breath unfurled in front of her like a dragon's.

"I read something in the encyclopedia," she said shyly as they watched the sky turn from orange to amber to gold. "It said when it's the first day of the midnight sun, the locals perform a special ceremony. I thought . . . I thought we could do it too?"

Dad didn't answer. So she hurried on. "They drink a shot of alcohol—obviously we wouldn't do that," she said hastily, feeling him tense beside her. "But I thought we could make some hot chocolate instead. They draw a big circle on the ground, a sacred circle they call it—it's meant to represent the sun, and they all stand inside and then make three wishes for the summer. It's said to bring good luck."

He stayed silent for the longest of times, but just

when she was about to go back inside, he clapped his hands together. "April. That is a wonderful suggestion. I'd better get the teapot on."

April giggled as Dad scurried indoors, his lanky arms pulling at everything in the kitchen at once—teapot, marshmallows, even some chocolate cookies—it didn't matter that a plate got broken or that the cupboard door almost came off its hinges or that half the hot chocolate ended up on the floor. With just minutes to spare before midnight, he reappeared outside and drew a huge circle in the ground with a wooden stick.

She finished off the circle with a few lines fanning outward like rays, and then they placed the teapot inside the circle and sat on some cushions borrowed from the sofa. The sun now hovered right on the edge of the horizon, the point where it normally would sink and disappear from sight before returning. But instead of vanishing, it remained stuck on the horizon like a basketball hoop, and around it, the colors in the sky turned from gold to bronze to apricot.

April took a big slurp of hot chocolate straight from the spout and couldn't remember being this happy for years.

"Three wishes," she said with a chocolaty sigh. "Don't forget to make them."

"Well, I have always wanted to see the midnight sun—ever since I first read about it when I was your age," Dad said. "Therefore, it feels like one of my wishes has come true already."

"But you can have two more!" said April, who had spent all three of her wishes already—one on Bear, one on Dad, and the final one on the planet.

She almost told Dad then. About Bear. It was on the tip of her tongue to tell him everything. She even opened her mouth, but somehow the words didn't form properly and then, when she had worked out her first sentence, it was too late. He had started speaking.

"It's Mom's birthday tomorrow," he said, so quietly she almost missed it. "And I'd always rather hoped she'd be with me, to see it together."

How could she have forgotten? A hot, fiery burst of shame flooded her veins. She reached out a hand to tentatively touch his arm, but with an apologetic shake of his head, Dad got up, brushed the dirt off his legs, and announced in a quiet voice that even though the sun was still in the sky, it was time for bed.

April picked up the teapot and the cushions and trudged into the cabin after him. The bedroom door was ajar, and she could see him standing by the record player, riffling through his records with flicks and shakes of his head. When he found the one he wanted, he sank back down into his bed.

"Good night, Dad," she called out.

But his record was already playing and he was lost to her. It was the sad piece—the one he played every year at this time. Later in bed, after about the hundredth play, she put her pillow over her head to block it out.

And still the sun kept shining.

11

THE WEATHER CABIN

IT WASN'T THAT APRIL didn't miss Mom, she mused the next morning over breakfast. It was just, if she were really honest, she could only really remember her in glimpses.

There'd been her bedtime stories. But also dancing in the backyard with sunshine the color of golden syrup, chocolate fudge cupcakes made for breakfast, and laughter that felt like popping candy. And there'd been hugs because that was the type of mom she was. Huggy.

And of course, there were the animal memories too. Sprinkling hedgehog food on the lawn at dusk and the three of them crouching indoors with the lights off to see who would spot the first one. Watching her mother feed robins from her hand while Dad looked on affectionately, and the time Mom rescued a tortoise that had wandered too far from home and Dad had teased her about wanting to keep it.

She sometimes wondered what life would have been like if Mom hadn't accidentally gotten hit by a car that day. Would April have been a bit more, well, normal? More like the other girls at school? They didn't play in backyards with foxes, or climb trees or talk to animals. She wasn't sure whether her differentness was because of her genes or just because of the way life had turned out.

She suspected a bit of both.

It wasn't Dad's fault. And it wasn't even that he didn't love her—it was just when Mom had died two achingly long days after the accident, she'd also taken half of Dad with her. Unfortunately, it was the half of him that was more fun. The Dad who used to sing when he saw a rainbow, who told silly jokes that made Mom snort with laughter, and definitely the half that didn't work so hard or snap when he got stressed. April glanced over at him where he sat slumped over the kitchen counter, the bags under his eyes almost falling into his cup of tea. His wild, unruly hair stuck up at right angles from his head, and his shirt was buttoned incorrectly.

Had he somehow thought he could escape his sadness by coming here? She sighed. Because he was wrong. Wherever he went, it seemed to follow him around like a comet trail.

"You ready?" Dad said, glancing at his watch impatiently.

"*Ready?*"

"To help me. You asked me the other day, don't you remember?"

"Yes. No." Oh. Fox poop. Why *today* of all days

should he suddenly want her help? What if Bear was waiting for her in Walrus Bay? She felt torn in two. Of course she wanted to spend time with Dad. Hadn't she been waiting for something like this ever since they got here? But she'd only suggested helping him out of frustration. She'd much rather do something fun together—like a game of soccer or sledding down the mountain or fishing in one of the lakes.

"April?" he said gently. "It was wrong of me to say you were too little to help me. On reflection, you're never too young to do important work. And it might even give you an idea for what you want to do when you grow up."

April nodded.

It was silly, of course. Because being grown up was so far away she might as well contemplate climbing into a spaceship and traveling to the moon.

Nevertheless, she mustn't forget that Dad was doing Very Important Work. Those reams and reams of dusty logbooks full of facts and figures going back to the first year since the meteorological station opened nearly a century ago. Sea temperatures, air temperatures, humidity, wind speed, and wind direction had all been measured since then and were now continuing to be measured by her father. Everyone had done such valuable work over the past hundred years, but it was perhaps never as essential as now.

April often wondered what she could do to help save the planet, and now here was her chance. So she pulled herself upright and followed him.

Whenever she entered the weather cabin, it was like walking into a different universe, a place full of strange mechanical instruments, ticking and humming in a neat, metallic way. She had the unsettling sensation they were inside a vacuum—when the door was closed, they were sealed off from the rest of the world and nothing else, not even Bear Island, could seep through. Inside, the air smelled dry and very slightly of aniseed.

"Why don't we measure the air temperature first?"

He explained why the air temperature was important in measuring how temperatures were shifting on a global scale, and how it was monitored. For this, they had to venture outside to the thermometer, which sat in the shade. It wasn't the usual kind of thermometer you would find at home. This one was bright red and about five feet high. There was a fairly complex series of readings to take, which Dad showed her how to do, and she recorded them in the logbook.

"How many people normally work here at any one time?" April asked after finishing her readings.

"Well," said Dad, frowning at the reading. "There always have to be two people on shift—just in case something happens to one of them. But they were so short staffed, they let me come with just you."

"Do you think they get much time off?"

"Time off?" Dad stared at her like she'd just spoken in a foreign language. 'There's no time off here.

Measuring the temperatures is a full-time job."

April chewed her lip in thought. "So no one would have had a chance to explore the island, then?"

"My dear girl. Is that what you want? You want me to spend more time with you?" He removed his glasses and rubbed his eyes tiredly. April was surprised to realize he might feel the same way as her. "It's just so hard with all these temperatures to take. I'll be honest . . . it's actually a lot more time-consuming than I imagined it would be, and especially by myself."

April opened her mouth to say something, but then she spotted how tense his shoulders were, and because she didn't want to add to his worries, she decided to bend the truth a little. "It's fine," she said. "I didn't mean it like that. I like exploring the island by myself. Actually today . . ."

If there were a perfect moment to tell him about Bear, now would be it. But apart from the fact that he had already turned back to his instruments and was once again frowning at them, what would she say? And even if she *did* tell him, how would he react? Was it worth the risk? Because if he knew there was a polar bear on the island, there's *no* way he'd let her be friends with him.

"I'm happy here," she said making her voice sound more confident than she felt. "*Really* happy."

They moved back inside the weather cabin to take the next set of temperatures. This part needed a lot more concentration, and Dad had to explain it three times. Unfortunately, he was not the most patient of teachers, and because one of the instruments was acting up and because he was stressed, he was even less so today. On each explanation, the lines between his eyes creased deeper and deeper in frustration, and she could tell he was getting bristly. No wonder. It was arduous, repetitive work.

Her eyes watered with all the effort, and her brain felt in danger of exploding. She had to keep reminding herself that she was doing Very Important Work. Dad was in here every day literally straining his eyes because it was absolutely crucial to measure the temperatures and record them accurately—this way people could get proof of how the temperatures were changing in the Arctic. After all, these changes would soon be affecting the whole planet, and who knew what would happen then? And even though this was something that made her desperately worried, every so often a sudden glimpse of Bear snuck into her mind and distracted her. She had told him she was coming back with food and some antiseptic cream for his paw, and she didn't like to think she was letting him down.

What if he was in pain? What if he felt like she had lied to him? What if she never saw him again? She hadn't even come close to figuring out how he had ended up stuck on the island, and the thought of him with his lonely, sad eyes and his head hung low and dejected flashed in her mind briefly. It was just a thought, but it was powerful enough to make her fingers tremble, and the red logbook she was holding ended up tumbling from her hands and falling facedown on the floor. Unfortunately, it also fell facedown on a splatter of tea Dad had spilled earlier.

"Oh no," she muttered, and tried to brush the tea off but just ended up smudging it across the page and making it even worse.

Dad rushed over and gazed at her in horror. There was an edge to his stare that made her want to shrink back inside herself and hide. Instead, he took the logbook from her, and with dismay, they both stared at the ruined page.

And that's when he finally snapped.

"What have you done?" he bellowed. "I knew I shouldn't have trusted you. You're just too little for this kind of work. You clumsy, stupid girl!"

As soon as his temper had burst, one of those horrible silences fell upon the cabin, and April had the strangest sensation that she was falling. There was nothing apart from the ticking and tocking of the instruments and the stale, fetid air of regret that lay heavy in the air.

"April!" Her father took a step toward her, guilt etched in every line of his face.

But it was too late.

Without looking back, she ran out the door, grabbed her backpack, and then sprinted all the way to Walrus Bay.

12

A SECRET SHARED

BY THE TIME APRIL got there, her hurt had almost all gone. Some of it had evaporated into the sea mist, and the rest had disappeared through the soles of her boots. The island had a way of making things seem less important, and within the past week, the sun had gently revealed the brackish gorse hiding under the melting snow.

Above her, a pack of gulls flew in a high arc across the sky, and something about the way they grouped together gave April a sudden, keen yearning for someone to talk to. Someone who would truly understand the remoteness of the island and this mysterious part of the world. The only person she could think of was Tör. But the thought of trudging back to the cabin, using the satellite phone, and facing Dad was just too much.

She told herself that he didn't mean it.

She knew most people didn't mean the things they said when they were shouting. Besides, arguments were bound to happen when confined to such a small place. Bear Island might be sixty-nine square miles, but at the same time, it might just as well be as large as the two cabins, given how much Dad explored outside of them.

She would forgive him because that was what she had always done. And what was the alternative? It wasn't like she could leave.

So it was she arrived in Walrus Bay, almost but not quite her sunshiny self. Just as she was wondering how long she would have to wait today and how Bear's paw was faring, she heard a loud splashing noise.

She turned around, and bounding out from the sea, shaking droplets of water everywhere as he galloped across the beach straight in her direction, was Bear. His exuberance and the way he bounced off the sand in sheer unbridled joy meant she started to run too, and so the pair of them sprinted across the beach toward each other.

"Bear!"

It was only when they were about five feet away from each other that they both ground to a halt, April feeling wary because here was a fully grown and potentially very dangerous polar bear, and yet at the same time slightly puzzled at what should happen next. What was the etiquette here? They couldn't shake hands, or hug or kiss cheeks the French way. She was still working it out when Bear rose up in the sky onto his rear legs and gave the most earsplitting, deafening roar possible.

And April, not even stopping to think about it, also

opened her mouth in the loudest roar she could make. Granted, it wasn't nearly as thunderous as Bear's, but it didn't matter. Not one jot. Because in that moment, she could easily forget everything else in the entire world.

And with the roar, any last bit of remaining hurt disappeared in a puff of magic.

So *that* was the way to greet a polar bear.

He dropped back to all fours and shook every last remaining droplet of water out of his white coat, spraying seawater, sand, and grit everywhere, but mostly all over April. She rubbed her face clean with her mitten, and when she could finally see again, she could have sworn Bear was grinning. "Hello, my friend."

Taking a couple of cautious steps closer, she saw again how desperately skinny he was and how his fur was dull and matted rather than a brilliant white. How his paws had turned slightly yellow—the same color as his teeth. The way his eyes were the exact same shade of dark chocolate as her hair. His tufty round ears—which were perhaps the most adorable part of him—danced with life and mischief. Those black whiskers, which, when he leaned forward, tickled her face and made her giggle. And then finally his nose, which was jet black and, when it touched her face, sniffing her in the way animals do, was cold and wet and made her laugh out loud.

"Why, you're not at all scary!" she exclaimed. "And yes, I *know* what you want. I've brought some peanut butter. But first I'd like to take a look at your paw, please?"

Even though she'd inspected it yesterday, April wasn't going to make any assumptions. An animal like Bear needed to be treated with respect at all times. Only when she was sure he was receptive did she gently crouch by his feet.

"Now, sit quietly for me. This won't take too long." The paw seemed less swollen today but still had raw patches where the plastic had dug into the skin. Because he was *so* huge, she had to use the entire tube of antiseptic cream to make sure she had covered all the damaged area. "That's it. I'll put some more on it tomorrow, but I think you'll be all right now."

With a sigh of relief, she sat back on her haunches. When Dad was talking about grown-up jobs, he often suggested a career as a vet for her. But the truth was, she just couldn't think of herself as someone who could ever put animals down.

"So saving you will do," she said. "Now, who wants some peanut butter?!"

Bear snorted and snuffled and nudged her shoulder impatiently.

"Wait!" she said. "I need to set the table first."

April removed a blanket from her backpack and laid it out next to the upturned boat, where the wind was less blowy. Then she placed the jar of peanut butter, the oat biscuits, and some dried raisins in the center. It didn't look like much of a picnic, especially for a starving polar bear, but it looked pretty and that would have to do. Understanding that food was in the offing, Bear sat on the cold shingle of the beach while April positioned herself on the blanket and turned to face him.

Was she too old for picnics? Fox poop. She'd never even been to a sleepover, let alone been part of a gang of best friends. And, she decided with a loud, satisfying crunch of her oat biscuit, she was going to make up for lost time.

"I know you're waiting!" she said. "Hold on."

Since Bear couldn't use a knife, she spread the peanut butter on for him in sloppy, fat dollops and laid the first oat biscuit next to his paw. Before she even had time to withdraw her hand, the biscuit was gobbled up. He ate fast, so fast, she didn't even think he chewed them—they just disappeared down his throat.

In the end, she gave him the entire box, and so he ate that too—cardboard included.

"You're still hungry?" She slid the half-full jar of peanut butter across the blanket, and for a second, she thought he was going to wolf down the entire thing, glass jar and all. But he stopped at the last moment and instead used his long pink tongue to extract every remaining scrap of peanut butter.

"I shall have to bring more food next time," she remarked, mentally scanning the provisions room and just how much food they actually had in there. "I'm sure Dad won't notice. He doesn't even like peanut butter anyway. I know! He's different from you and me. He's a bit different from everyone, really. But he can't help it."

Bear pawed the empty jar, preoccupied with finding more food, but finding none, he looked up and studied April quizzically.

Talking about Dad made her remember how he'd shouted at her. Not with any hurt—that had all gone, but with a sense of sadness.

"The thing is, I know he wasn't angry with me. Not deep down anyway. He's under pressure with this job, but it's not that either." She looked up. Bear's attention had been caught by something out to sea, but knowing he wasn't facing her made it easier to talk somehow. "You know the real reason he was angry? It's because it's been seven years since Mom died, but it might just as well have been yesterday."

She followed Bear's gaze, where the waves slammed and crashed against the shore in hard, wrathful gasps. Seven years and Dad was angry because he still had an emotion inside of him so big, so vast, and so bottomless that it came out in lots of different ways. He was angry because he missed his wife, and even though Granny Apples thought that it was self-indulgent and that he should be over it by now, he wasn't.

April turned back to Bear to find him staring at her. "And sometimes," she whispered, "sometimes I don't think he ever will be."

Bear cocked his head, attuned to the changes in tone of her voice as if sensing she had something important to say. "I wish . . . ," she started, but then stopped and pulled a loose thread on her mitten. "I wish . . . I wish he could meet a new wife," she said at last. "I know it's bad of me to say that because I had my mom. To be honest, I can't remember much about her except she was made of rainbows. But the thing is, she's not here anymore and I think Dad is lonely and it would help him to meet someone new. Someone lovely, of course. Not rainbows—not everyone can be made of rainbows—but someone just as nice."

A gull screeched loudly overhead, and eventually she dared herself to look up. She'd never said any of this out loud before. Would Bear be disappointed in her? He couldn't understand exactly what she was saying, but it seemed to April that he didn't appear to be angry. His eyes were even softer, like the gooey chocolate you find in the middle of a warm brownie, and he wore the kind of expression that encouraged her to speak, to share her secrets and to unburden herself.

She took a deep breath.

"Yes . . . there is something I'm not saying." She yanked the thread so it came away in her hand, before spinning away in the wind. "You see things, don't you, Bear? You see things that are unspoken. I'm a bit like that too. I think it comes from spending so much time alone. So, yes, it's not just for Dad." She gulped. "It's for me too. I . . . *I* wouldn't mind a new mom. Someone to make the house warm when I come home from school, who'll ask me all sorts of questions about my day and maybe even take me to a real hairdresser once in a while."

In the silence that followed, the sea crashed onto the

beach, the island hummed to its own current, and the sun disappeared and then reappeared behind a cloud. April drew her knees up to her chest to cover her raw, beating heart and pressed her face against her knees.

She had said too much.

She hadn't meant to. The words had just spiraled out of her. And now she couldn't take them back. They had already been whipped away by the wind and were somewhere out there. And they would be out there forever now. What if they reached the cabin? What if *that* happened? What if—her breath skittled furiously against her rib cage—what if Dad had heard her? She would never be able to forgive herself if she had hurt him with her words.

These kinds of horrible, nasty thoughts rattled through her mind, and the awful churning in her stomach felt worse than during any exam, worse than the time the girls had laughed at her at school, worse even than when she'd seen a dead cat on the road.

April rubbed her eyes, and without realizing she was doing it, she found herself leaning into Bear's soft fur. He shifted slightly at the movement but didn't move away, and so she leaned her cheek against his shoulder and let it gently rest there.

NO MORE SCHOOL!

WHEN APRIL HAD A CHANCE to think about it, she realized Bear probably didn't understand what she was saying. Not the *details* anyway. But sometimes—maybe often—the details weren't important. It was the feeling behind them that mattered.

And in that moment, Bear had seemed to sense something about her, the way animals are uncanny about sensing the things humans fail to see. Hadn't she read about how cats know when a storm is coming? Or how horses pick up your fear? Or dogs who can read your emotions from just one look on your face? Animals were smart like that. Not academic smart—they wouldn't pass any exams. But they read the world—and the people in it—in a different way.

They read the world with their feelings.

And April just knew Bear had read her feelings perfectly. In a way that Dad had been unable to read them for years. Better even than Granny Apples, who, in her well-meaning but slightly clumsy way, sometimes got it wrong.

As the sunlight settled around the island in warm apricot hues, April skipped home. There was no sign of life in the cabin other than the glowing embers of the fire and a silence that felt thick and gloopy.

Was Dad asleep?

She paused at his bedroom door, her hand hovering nervously over the handle, but she wasn't brave enough to enter. Instead, she tiptoed into her bedroom and noiselessly closed the door behind her. It was only when she reached the bed that she noticed the teapot on the floor.

"Oh."

She picked it up and opened the lid. The aroma of hot chocolate floated out like galloping unicorns. Even though it had gone tepid, April still drank it straight out of the spout until it had all disappeared. And that night she had the best, deepest, most velvety night's sleep since arriving.

★

Come morning—at least she thought it was morning; it was hard to tell when there was no night to break the daylight—April lay in bed with the covers pulled up to her nose. Although she had gotten used to the cold, the mornings were still the worst. Instead of getting up, she shivered under the covers and drew some connect-the-dots in the air to make sense of how a polar bear had ended up on Bear Island and yet absolutely no one seemed to have noticed.

She had so far concluded:

- From her conversation with Dad, it was obvious that previous meteorologists simply hadn't had the time to explore the island.
- In this way, it had been relatively easy for Bear to stay on the far side of the island and remain undetected.
- He must have seen human beings before, but only from a distance.
- Although he seemed fully grown, there was also something young about him. Polar bears could live up to about twenty years. So perhaps he was about her age, or younger?
- But she still didn't know how long he'd been here.
- And, if the ice caps around Bear Island had melted, how he had gotten here at all?

There was only one thing to do, and that was to find

out. She didn't know how and she didn't know when, but she would get to the bottom of it.

But first—she pricked her ear for any sign of music—it was time to get up. With teeth bared, she leaped out of bed and hurriedly pulled on her clothes. The weather changed rapidly here, which had something to do with the island being buffeted by three different weather fronts, but one thing was for certain—it was always cold. Once dressed in all her layers, she was almost twice the size, and she waddled out into the living room.

Good. Dad wasn't up yet. As the cabin was liable to be as chilly as outside, they needed fire. This was normally Dad's job, but being a practical type, she had often made the fire back home, and so this morning she coaxed the flames into life. She then flicked the kettle on, washed out his mug, and put his favorite jar of marmalade out. She even dusted the kitchen counter and swept the floor.

When Dad emerged from his bedroom, wearing his best suit, he asked her which Mozart album she preferred to accompany breakfast. He then offered to do *all* the dishes—there were a few empty soup cans, saucepans, and spoons that had gathered in the sink. Most miraculous of all, he even offered to put a load of laundry in.

"April . . . ," he said once his first cup of coffee had been diligently drunk. She looked up and Dad's face colored. He ummed and ahhed and cleared his throat a few times. Then, after another throat clear, he slid across his allocated three aniseed candies for the day. "Here, these are for you."

She took the candy in her hand. They weren't her favorite, but she appreciated the gesture all the same. April sometimes wondered about other families who just said sorry and if this was easier or harder. But since she had no concept of that, she didn't think about it too hard. This was just the way it was.

However, she did have one question. And now was the perfect time to ask it.

"Dad?"

"Yes, April?"

"Since it's *technically* the start of summer now, does that mean I still have to go to school?"

"Well . . . um . . . I'm not sure," he said, distracted by his second cup of coffee, which was still too hot to drink. "It seems a tad early, does it not? To break up for the end of the school year?"

"Early for my school back home, yes," she answered. "But not too early for Norway. See here." She jabbed her finger at the open page in the encyclopedia she had prepared in advance. "Schools in Norway finish much earlier. It has to do with the weather."

He looked slightly befuddled, with marmalade caught on his whiskers and a puzzled frown. "I . . .well, that is to say . . ."

April held her breath. He was about to say no—the

word was already floating around the room like a nasty smell, but in the end, as she hoped it would, guilt won.

"Yes. I can't see why not." He offered a watery smile. "When in Norway . . . or at least, in Norwegian territories."

He never bothered to look at the open page—for which April was glad, because she had, in fact, omitted a small detail. She hadn't lied, exactly, because schools in Norway did finish earlier.

Just not *this* early.

"So that's it, then?" she asked, snapping the encyclopedia shut. "No more school."

Dad picked up his still-too-hot coffee and slurped loudly. Before he had even put his mug back down, April had skipped out of the door humming her happy song.

Which went something like this:

"I'm happy, happy, HAPPY.

So, so, so, SO happy.
I'm full of sunshine and smiles.
I'm not even afraid of crocodiles!
I'm happy, happy, HAPPY."

And for good measure, she finished it off with a bear roar.

14

BEAR RIDE

NO MORE SCHOOL.

No more school! It could only mean one thing, April thought as she danced and twirled and bounced across the island. Summer had truly begun!

Bear obviously had the same thought in mind, because when she arrived at Walrus Bay, he was rolling around on the sand having a good back rub—looking the happiest she had yet seen him. As she watched him, her tummy danced with excitement that she should be sharing the island with such a magnificent creature.

"I'm here!" she shouted out, and Bear jumped to his feet, shook off the sand, and galloped toward her, the sheer force of him almost knocking her off her feet. "Hello."

After a brief hesitation, he leaned forward, and with only the teeniest hint of nerves, she allowed him to sniff her face, which—apart from a welcome roar— seemed to be his way of saying hello back. A wet nose rub against her seven freckles and a sloppy lick of her nose.

"Aaaargh, your breath!" she gasped, pulling back.

After quickly tending to his paw, which looked so much better, she doled out four packs of oat biscuits, two jars of peanut butter, and the three aniseed candies Dad had given her. Bear gobbled them all up in seconds.

"What have you been living on here?" she asked softly. "Why are you here all alone?"

April waited for answers, but there was nothing other than his wet nose pressing into her hand for oat biscuit crumbs.

—

"Don't worry. Now that your paw is healed, you can go hunting again." April had spotted a few seals dotted on the rocks around the island but also knew that polar bears relied on the ice as a kind of platform to help catch them. There must be other things that polar bears could hunt, although April wasn't one hundred percent sure what they were. "Don't worry, I'll make sure you have enough peanut butter to eat too."

Bear licked the last of the crumbs and then settled by her side, his warm body ever so slightly touching hers. With their backs resting against the upturned boat, April contemplated how to spend their time.

"We've got the *whole* summer, Bear. What do you say to that?! That's the rest of May, then *all* of June, July, and August and September! That's like THIS much time." She opened her arms to their widest possible span. Bear looked at her perplexed. Admittedly, her span wasn't nearly as big as his. "It's still a lot, though. But first today. We've got the whole day ahead of us."

Bear seemed to understand that one and bared his teeth in what could, just about, be recognized as a grin. Either that or he was just yawning.

"Right—what shall we do, then?" She flapped her hand in excitement. "I know! Let's go exploring!"

She sprang to her feet, and following suit, Bear slowly lumbered to all fours. She didn't know where exactly to go exploring but set off toward the trio of mountains anyway in short, confident steps. But when she looked back, Bear had turned the other way and was loping in the opposite direction in long, loping paces.

April gazed forlornly at his retreating hindquarters. "Where are you going?"

Bear didn't break his stride but instead looked back over his shoulder. It was all the encouragement she needed, and she raced after him.

"Hold on!" she cried. "You'll have to walk slower than that."

Unfortunately, however slow Bear walked, it was still *way* faster than April's fastest walk. It was even worse than walking with Dad, who always took one stride to her every four steps. They continued like this for about ten minutes. But it was no use. Either Bear was ahead, waiting impatiently for her to catch up, or she was out of breath running to keep up with him.

When her lungs were ragged and her sides bursting, she ground to a halt as Bear leaped over yet another inland pond as easily if he were jumping over puddles. She'd managed to jump the first few, but this one was much wider.

"Bear!" she shouted, but her voice was whipped back in her face by the wind, and he was fast disappearing. Too long to walk around, there was no choice—she was going to have to just jump. With a deep breath, she hurled herself into the air, but as soon she took off, she knew she'd made a mistake. And with a horrible thud, she landed half in, half out of the water and felt her ankle fold.

She gasped in shock.

The water was cold and slapped against her feet. Thank goodness for her waterproof trousers. She clawed her way out and collapsed on her side in a breathless, soggy heap. Bear was nowhere to be seen, and a shimmer of unease passed through her. Where exactly was she? And more important, how would she get home? She tried testing her ankle, and a sharp pain shot up her leg.

So much for the first day of summer vacation. It was silly to think she could be friends with a polar bear anyway—let alone try to help him. What had she been imagining? He was a wild animal, and she was just a little girl. A little girl who couldn't even jump across a pond.

April sank her face in her hands and tried not to feel too sorry for herself.

It was then he reappeared. So quietly she didn't even notice until he stood ten feet away with the enormous shadow of his head resting on her lap.

"Bear?"

He was outlined against the sun, so all she could see was his silhouette. "I was trying too hard to keep up and I fell over," she explained, pointing to her ankle. "I don't think it's broken. Just twisted. But I can't walk very well."

Bear didn't move. Naturally, he didn't understand, but curiosity brought him closer until he was standing right over her.

"I can't come any farther," she said. "I'm so sorry."

She didn't really know why she was apologizing, only that she felt sad inside, like she had ruined their day. Bear brought his nose closer and licked some of the wet off her trousers. He couldn't have known where she was hurt, but it seemed he licked her ankle extra gently, just how Dad used to clean her grazes when she fell off her bike.

"Thank you, Bear." She felt a sudden prick of emotion. "That feels much better now."

She was wondering how on earth she was going to get home, and trying her best not to worry, when he nudged her shoulder. "What is it?" He nudged her shoulder again, this time more forcibly. "I can try to move, but look." She got to her feet and winced as she put weight on her ankle. "I'll be too slow."

She sat back down again and put on her bravest face. Bear sank to his belly so he was her height and looked at her expectantly.

"What is it, Bear?"

He continued to gaze at her, and something shivery ran through her veins. He couldn't possibly mean what she thought he meant. . . .

"You want me to get on?" she exclaimed. "But I've

never even been horseback riding, let alone *bear* riding. Oh my!"

Could this *really* be happening? She closed her eyes against the glare of the sun and then opened them again. But Bear was still there, crouched in front of her, waiting.

There was nothing else she could do. If she didn't get on, she'd be stuck out here. She had to stop being such a wimp. Taking a deep, steadying breath, April grabbed a handful of fur by his neck and slid her left leg over. Under her bottom, she could feel his jagged rib cage.

"Oh, Bear," she murmured. "Are you sure you can carry me?"

Bear roared indignantly and rose in one majestic swoop. She wobbled from side to side but just about managed to hold on until he stood upright on all four paws. She gazed at the island from her new vantage point and couldn't help but think it was a bit like sitting on a throne.

"This is fun!"

But as soon as the words were out of her mouth, Bear sprinted forward, and she was flung to the left, then tossed to the right, and then hurled back to the left before a huge lurch to the right. The wind gushed past her ears like sails, the ground heaved and rolled, and worst of all she had absolutely nothing to hold on to apart from the tufts of fur around his neck, which kept slipping out of her hands.

In the end, she stretched her arms around his neck, pressed her cheek to his fur, and clung on. That way, if she kept her eyes tightly shut, her bottom didn't bounce quite so much, her rib cage didn't rattle quite as loudly, and her stomach wasn't threatening to empty its contents.

After a bit, it was quite warming too.

Bear's steady pulse beat against her skin, and there was something about it that felt both comforting and safe. Like coming home after a day at school to a house smelling of freshly baked chocolate cupcakes.

If the girls in her class could see her now. They wouldn't laugh then, would they? No. Because while *they* were stuck in boring old school, April Wood was galloping across a wild, uninhabited island on the back of a polar bear.

15

THE CAVE

THE RIDE COULD HAVE lasted five minutes or five hours.
However long it took—and April wasn't counting—it
was timeless. In all her life, she knew she would never
ever forget this moment. When it finally ended, she
slid off Bear's body and sensed, deep in her soul, that
things could never go back to how they were before.

There were no words to thank him, so she wrapped
her arms around his neck and squeezed him tight. Not
too hard in case she unsettled him, but tight enough
to let him feel the soft beating of her heart.

"Oh, Bear," she whispered, resting her face against
his fur.

When she finally let go, he loped off back in the direction of Walrus Bay, and April watched until he became smaller and smaller and eventually disappeared from sight. Then she shook herself, looked around, and realized she wasn't too far from the cabin and was able to hobble the rest of the way home by herself.

★

Even though it was boring being stuck indoors, April sensibly rested in the cabin for a few days until her ankle had fully recovered. But as soon as it was better, she raced back to Walrus Bay armed with some food. With a sigh of relief, she was pleased to see Bear was waiting for her, and so she treated him with an extra jar of peanut butter.

Over the next few weeks, as May turned into June, she tried to take as much food as she could from the storeroom without arousing suspicion. This wasn't too hard, given that Dad's head was buried deep in his work, and these days he barely noticed if April was there or not. The only problem was how much Bear ate. It was way more than she ate, or her father ate, or anyone she'd ever known before to eat. The storeroom only had a finite amount of food, whereas Bear had a bottomless stomach, and however much she fed him, he still gazed at her with his chocolate eyes and implored her for more.

Standing by the upturned boat at Walrus Bay, which had become their daily meeting point, she stood and watched as he galloped toward her. The good news was that all this extra food was starting to show. His coat had become noticeably less matted, his hip bones no longer jutted out quite so much, and when she rode him (which never failed to fill her with awe), the vertebrae had almost disappeared under a thick, broad back made up of sinew and muscle. And the best bit was his fur. With all the additional food on top of his existing diet, it had become extra soft, like the kind of fleece blanket you snuggle into on the sofa. He smelled of toasted marshmallows, chestnuts, and hot buttered pancakes. And if she buried her nose, she even fancied she could taste peanut butter on her tongue.

After he had eaten everything she had brought, he spent another minute or so sniffing her pockets just in case he had missed any.

"No more," she said. "We have to ration it out from now on."

He looked at her questioningly and nudged her hand in hope.

"Anyway," she said. "You still haven't shown me where you live. You know so much about me, but there's still so many things I don't know about you!"

Bear seemed perplexed. She wasn't sure if his expression meant he'd understood her or that he was still hungry. Either way, when he eventually realized there was no more food to come, April was able to climb aboard, and once she was in place, he set off toward the smallest of the three mountains, although it was still incredibly steep. April had to close her eyes because looking down the side of a mountain was far worse than any roller coaster she'd ever been on—and this was without any safety harness. But she needn't have worried. Bear climbed with the gracefulness of a tiger all the way to a tight, narrow ledge about halfway up before coming to standstill outside a medium-sized cave in the side of the mountain.

Bear's home.

April had to flatten herself along his back so the pair of them could enter. Inside, the cave opened up, and she was able to slide off his back and stand upright. Of course, she could barely see a thing and had no idea how far the cave stretched back. But it was sheltered from the elements and made the perfect hiding place.

"But it's not very cozy, is it?" She squinted her eyes to try to adjust to the lack of light. Bear, being huge and white, wasn't hard to miss, but the rest of the cave was shrouded in a gloomy, damp darkness. In the corner, she could just about make out a small pile of feathers, eggshells, and bones, although it wasn't something she wanted to look at too closely. At least it explained how he sourced his food. But what a life. The whole cave smelled moldy, and she couldn't help but shudder. She reached out and stroked his muzzle. Even though the encyclopedia said male polar bears preferred to be solitary (apart from when they wanted to find a mate or get into the occasional fight), she couldn't help but feel sorry for him. "You poor thing. How long have you been living here all alone?"

Bear growled under his breath. It was not a happy, contented growl but more of an angry, frustrated one. A growl that spoke not of months—but of *years*. The very thought of him stuck in this cave, with no chance of meeting any of his own kind, was almost unbearable.

"How did you end up trapped here on the island?"

He growled again, and for a moment, Bear's story hovered unspoken between them, like something tremulous and alive in the air.

April held her breath.

But then, whatever the story was and wherever it had come from, it disappeared like a puff of smoke. Bear shook his head vigorously from side to side, and by instinct, they headed toward the cave entrance, where at once the air felt clean and light.

In the sudden, radiant bask of the sun, which coated their faces like honey, Bear turned to April and licked her face from top to bottom. And because his breath was so bad and because it was so unexpected and because his tongue was so wet, April started to giggle. It was the kind of laughter that follows a sad moment—big, loud, and full of relief. She laughed and laughed so hard that she tumbled onto her back and clutched her tummy to stop it hurting. And then Bear rolled next to her and he lay on his back, and his ears were twitching and it was like he was laughing too.

They lay like that in the mouth of the cave, laughing. "Oh, Bear," she managed to say at last. "I do love you."

He couldn't say the words *I love you*, but he didn't need to.

It was there in the warm, comforting weight of his body next to hers, in the way he gazed at her with such naked open trust with those melted-chocolate eyes. It was there unspoken between them, and it would be there forever.

Love, she decided, was like magic.

She leaned over and put her arms around his neck for a cuddle. "Whatever it was that made you sad, you can tell me one day, Bear," she murmured into his fur. "I've been through sad things myself, so don't worry about upsetting me. I'll understand."

Bear's ears twitched gently, and he leaned his head into her embrace.

"You just tell me whenever you're ready. That's the best time to tell a story. Not before and not after. But only when it's ready to come out." She leaned into him even closer and kissed his face. "And . . . I promise I'll try to make it better for you."

And this time when he roared, it bounced off the cave walls and thudded straight into her heart.

16

LESSONS IN ROAR

THE REST OF THE DAY they spent exploring. First, he took her to the farthest corners in the east, where they stood at the very edge of the island, on top of some jagged cliffs that fell down into the violent gray waves. And even though they stood right near the edge and were buffeted this way and that by angry sea-rush winds, April never felt unsafe—not with Bear guarding and protecting her. She could never be unsafe with him.

"I want to learn to roar like you do!" she shouted over the waves.

Luckily she didn't have too long to wait to watch and learn. Bear reared up on his hind legs and bellowed out the kind of thunderous roar that skimmed over the waves like rocks and eventually melted into the faraway distance.

She tried to do the same, but her own roar belly-flopped into the sea with a big fat splat. Bear showed her how to puff out her chest, stand as tall as she possibly could—and then taller—and let the roar travel up all the way from her core so it came from the deepest, wildest part of her.

Her second roar was a little better but still not nearly as deafening as Bear's. She practiced and practiced until April looked at her watch and realized it was past eleven. But she didn't feel at all tired. That was the thing with all this sunshine. Without darkness, there was nothing to make you sleepy.

"I ought to go home all the same," she said. "But we can come back tomorrow, can't we? And I can try again?"

She took Bear's ear twitch as agreement. And so

they came back almost every day after that to practice her roar. And with each roar, she became a little bit more bear and a little bit less human. It didn't matter how small she was. It only mattered how much she wanted to be heard.

It wasn't just all roaring. As he continued to grow in strength, he took her all the way to the most westerly point in the island, where the land shelved into the sea in gigantic, weather-beaten boulders and rough, pointy shards of rocks jutted out of the water like knives.

"I didn't know this was here, Bear," she breathed out in wonder. "This is so beautiful! But . . . you're not going to jump onto the boulders, are you? Oh! You are!"

By now, riding Bear was becoming easier—especially if she dug her knees into his muscular flanks and held in her belly for balance. She clung on tight as he soared from boulder to boulder, as if they were mere stepping stones, and he jumped farther and farther out into the sea while all the time, the freezing water snapped at her heels. Dad's warning not to go too close to the sea's edge popped into her head, but she dismissed it. After all, he had said he didn't want her going too close to the sea's edge alone.

But she wasn't alone, was she?

"Catch me if you can, waves!" She shrieked with laughter as Bear jumped even higher.

Another day—perhaps it was the next day, or the one after, or even the one after that—Bear took her inland, where, with all his newfound energy, he leaped through the shiny blue lakes like he was skipping through puddles. He stopped by one lake in particular with vivid blue water the color of the summer sky.

"A lake in the shape of a heart!" April crouched by the water's edge and ran her fingers through the cold, crystal water. Their reflections gazed back at them hazily—shimmering and dancing and somehow as alive and breathless as they were. "A heart-shaped lake just for us. Look how small I am compared to you! I'm tiny," she said. "But we make a good pair, don't we, Bear? We make the *best* pair."

And Bear nuzzled her shoulder.

As June turned into July, he showed her the side of the island where tiny purple flowers had sprung into bloom. Then he took her higher up the mountain, where the snow still lay in thick, cold layers because even though it was summer, it was still almost freezing. More than once, April even brought the sled, and she whizzed down the mountain with a yell of laughter. She was doing all the things she had longed to do when she first heard they were coming to the Arctic Circle, and her heart soared as high as the sky in happiness. Another day, they collected all the litter in Walrus Bay, and Bear helped drag the sled back home—making sure not to be seen by Dad.

There was no part of the island they did not visit.

Together, they discovered every secret, every nook, every cranny, every edge, every side, every single inch of the island. They explored all the lakes, all the caves, all the mountains, and all the streams. They explored all the beaches on the island. The sandy ones, the pebbly ones, the ones that didn't even look like beaches, the hidden ones and the one where Dad and April had first landed. Not that she thought much about that day. All that was as distant in her memory as her old life back home. Like some hazy mirage she couldn't quite believe had existed at all.

One afternoon right at the beginning of August, she was sitting cross-legged in Walrus Bay while Bear played in the waves. He disappeared under the surface before emerging with whiskers dripping with seawater. He looked so different these days. It wasn't just that his coat was a brilliant shiny white, or that he radiated the kind of raw power only an animal can give off; it was the fact he was happy. Even though April had never met any other polar bears, she knew how to spot happiness—he held his head at a jaunty angle, waggled his nose, and rolled around on his back with his legs in the air and squirmed. And even though it had been a huge risk, April felt so deliciously glad that she had ignored Tör's warning and listened to her own instincts instead.

"I'm happy too," she said with a matching grin. "I don't have whiskers that I can shake, but I *am* happy. You know, Bear. I think I'm the happiest I've *ever* been."

The days continued to pass, marked only with the iridescent shine of happiness. There was no dusk, and there was no dawn. Even her watch stopped. It had something to do with being so close to the North Pole. And with nothing to tell the time, day blended into night and night blended into day. Time was no longer hands on a clock but something endless, infinite and magical.

It was summer.

And it was the *best* summer.

17

THE ISLAND SPEAKS

BUT IF THERE WAS ONE cloud on the horizon, then it was the kind of cloud that grew darker no matter how long the sun shone. Because the more Bear returned to his full strength, the more April worried. It wasn't just that she couldn't imagine saying goodbye to him. She couldn't even contemplate *that*. This was far worse. Because what would happen to him once she was gone? How would he survive all by himself in that dark, dank lonely cave for months or even years more?

These were questions that gnawed at her when she was apart from him, and they were especially loud and fearful when she was in bed. For no matter how much she tossed and turned, she couldn't think of the answers. Because even though he could feed himself now that his paw had healed, the truth was Bear didn't belong here.

This wasn't his home.

The more April thought about it, the more it became clear that he couldn't possibly stay here. But what to do about it? The answer, she decided one sleepless night, lay in finally discovering how he had ended up on the island in the first place.

★

The next day, determined to get some answers, she hurried to Walrus Bay as soon as she got up. She was early and Bear wasn't even there yet, so she whistled. It wasn't just a through-the-teeth one. It was a proper two fingers in her mouth whistle she had learned from watching the fishermen near Granny Apples's house.

It didn't matter that it wasn't the loudest whistle

either, because wherever Bear was on the island, he could still hear her. He was attuned to her in the way animals develop a sixth sense about the people they love. Thirty seconds later, she spotted his familiar figure on the horizon.

"Over here!" She waved, thrusting a tin of oily mackerel his way when he arrived. "No peanut butter today. You can have this instead." Worryingly, the jars of peanut butter had been going down rapidly, as had their other provisions. In fact, the storeroom had less than a quarter of their food remaining. Luckily, Dad never went in there, so hadn't noticed but it was another concern ticking away in her head.

Bear ended up eating the mackerel cold straight from the tin. Afterward he gave a satisfied belch.

"I've brought some things to show you today," she said, trying not to wince at the smell of his breath. "I thought you might like to see them."

April spread her picnic blanket out and sat cross-legged upon it while Bear sat licking his lips on the shingle. "See, this is my heart-shaped pebble. It's from the beach near Granny Apples's house, and I always sleep with it under my pillow for good luck. And this is a photo of my mom and dad. It was taken on their wedding day. Yes, you're right. He does look very smiley here." She gazed at the photo. She'd looked at it thousands of times before, but under Bear's watchful gaze, it was as if her old eyes had been removed and she was seeing it for the first time. "He actually has a nice smile, doesn't he? It's in his eyes. The way they crinkle at the edges like stars."

Bear's ears twitched, and April liked to think it was in agreement.

"I . . . I just wish Dad would smile at me like that these days." She sighed, one of those sighs that come from a very deep place, and it took a moment to find her voice again. "I had hoped this summer might bring us closer together," she said quietly. "But it hasn't. If anything, it's driven us further apart than ever." Since April didn't know how to make things better with Dad, she lifted her chin, shook the bad thoughts out of her head, and only then remembered why she'd rushed to the bay today in the first place. "You know, Bear. I wish I knew your story too. You're here all alone, but you must have a mom and dad like me." She looked at Bear's face expectantly, but his expression didn't change.

It wasn't like she expected him to reply. She simply hoped for some kind of sign that would help her make sense of his background. But Bear just yawned, flopped onto his front paws, and closed his eyes. She exhaled slowly, then leaned forward and rubbed the space between his ears. She wouldn't give up—she just needed to find the key to unlocking his history.

As he dozed, she sat watching him. It might seem strange to other people to just watch an animal sleep.

But actually, April knew it to be one of the most special gifts an animal could give a human, because it showed how much Bear trusted her. She'd been able to tell him all her deepest, most innermost feelings, and having a confidant was such a new feeling. She could literally tell Bear *anything* in the whole wide world, and he had never once laughed at her or made her feel silly.

All in all, he was the best friend she'd ever had.

When he finally woke up with a loud yawn, she hopped onto his back, and then they galloped halfway up the middle-sized mountain, where she showed him how to make snowballs, bunched up tight in her fists like golf balls, and how to chuck them at one another. They made some snow angels, then spent the lunchtime practicing her roar, and the afternoon learning how to smell the air.

You had to really inhale deeply. She didn't have his nose, but after weeks of practicing, she had finally managed to smell the hard ice of the glaciers in the North Pole. They smelled sharp and clean, like glass bottles. He also showed her how to tell which way the wind was blowing, and if there was snow coming, or a storm due or even rain in the air.

Best of all on this particular afternoon, he taught her to listen. Not just listen like you and I listen. But *really* listen. When she cocked her head and opened her ears, she could hear snowflakes settle on the mountaintops, the creaks and groans of cargo ships out of sight, and even Dad's sighs on the breeze. Then, when the sleet had cleared and the sun reappeared and they couldn't tell if was afternoon, evening, or even the next day, he taught her how to listen to the island itself.

Of course, at first she had no idea what he was doing. She'd watched curiously as he lay flat on the ground with his ear pressed to the earth. Long seconds passed, and the only sound was the gentle exhalation of her own breath.

"What are you listening to?" she asked at last.

With no answer forthcoming, the only thing to do was to find out for herself.

She copied the way Bear had flattened himself on the ground and lay with her own ear pressed to the earth. At first, she didn't hear anything other than her own hot breath or the wind in her ears or the sound of the waves in the distance. But after a few minutes, she did start to hear something else. Something separate from all of that. Something that was coming up from the center of the Earth itself.

"I can hear!" she gasped. "I can hear the island!"

It sounded like the noise you hear when you hold a shell to your ear. Or the wind in your ears when you're on roller coaster. Or the whisper of trees in a faraway magical land.

"It's beautiful!"

She lay with her ear pressed to the ground for hours. It was a bit like falling asleep in a hammock, and just as April was dozing off, the island did something funny.

It sighed.

Her ears pricked up.

Islands couldn't sigh, could they? She listened harder. There it was again. A sigh. But not a happy sigh of contentment—the kind you make after eating your birthday meal or a whole bar of white chocolate. It was the *other* kind of sigh. The kind of sigh adults make when they watch the news, open bank statements, or pick up the phone only to hear bad news.

That kind of sigh.

April shivered and sat up. She squeezed her nose and blew hard. But the sound of the island was still ringing in her ears.

"Bear?" She looked across anxiously. "Did you hear that?"

He raised himself from the ground and slowly turned around to face her. She was finally about to discover why Bear had ended up trapped on the island.

18

MOUNTAIN SUMMIT

BEFORE SHE COULD UNDERSTAND how it even happened, she was on Bear's back, and they were galloping toward a part of the island they'd only visited a couple of times before—approaching the mountains from a direction they had never traveled before, where icy streams tumbled and fell toward the sea and the gorse was thick and purple. As Bear jumped over lakes, colonies of gulls took flight and scattered into the air. To the right of them, the gray waves tossed and turned, and somewhere way in the distance, an arctic fox scampered away in fright.

Up close, the mountains were made of steel-colored

granite, stark and imposing and very, very tall. Everywhere was awash with gulls, squawking, screaming, screeching, shrieking. Scattering this way and that as Bear galloped straight through them and headed directly toward the biggest, steepest, most menacing mountain of all.

And then he started to climb.

The mountain was steep. So steep in places that April clung on for dear life lest she slide off and tumble all the way back down. So steep that at times it felt like they would have to turn back. There was just *no* way he could go on.

But on he did go. Onward and upward.

It was testament to his brute strength, his determination, or just his inner courage. They climbed and scrambled and clawed until they were nearly at the summit, a precarious point of snowcapped rock barely larger than the cabin. A sharp needle that cut into the blue sky. Surely there was no way Bear could climb this final part? The rock reared above them like an impassable granite wall. Her heart spun in her chest, her fingers clung on so tight her knuckles started to ache.

Bear slowed momentarily. He lowered on his haunches, took a powerful deep breath right down into his soul, and then leaped—he leaped through the sky as he soared to the summit.

And time stopped.

There was nothing but this moment. This one precious, beautiful, suspended moment. When she clung onto Bear. When Bear clung onto her. And when the pair of them flew through the sky. Everything was drenched in silence, the silence of Big Momentous Things.

The moment lasted forever, maybe even a lifetime.

During this endless time, lots of thoughts ran through April's head. How the summit seemed to stay achingly out of reach. How the bottom of the mountain looked an awfully long way down. How, despite her fear, she instinctively trusted Bear with her life. Most of all, how this had been the best, most perfect summer of her life. And something else that wasn't even a thought at all because thoughts weren't really made for this kind of thing. It was a feeling.

She was flying.

And it was like no feeling on earth.

It was clouds dancing across the sky. Planets out of reach, shooting stars, and sparkly, glittering comets.

It was *magnificent*.

Just as she was getting used to the weightlessness—the air rushing past her ears and the feeling of being a bird—they landed on the summit with a giant thump. Bear's front paws skidded in the snow. Pebbles dislodged and tumbled over the edge and clattered to their death on the rocks below. He shuddered and heaved and panted and finally collapsed onto his belly. His breath made shapes in the still, sharp air.

April slid off, landing on the snow with a soft bump, her legs aching, her hands sore from holding on so tight, her ears burning, but her heart shining and bursting with life.

For a moment, she lay flat on her back catching her breath. The sky above was close enough to touch. She was so high up! The highest up she had ever been without being in an airplane. She was so high her head was swimming and in her mouth was the taste of something she hardly recognized.

She twisted her head one way and saw the whole of the island spread below her like a tapestry. The hundreds of lakes looked like vivid blue patches. Walrus Bay stretched out like a sandy smile in the distance. And way, way to the south, two small red dots that were the meteorological station.

When she twisted her head the other way, all she could see was sea. Sea, sea, and more sea. They really were just a speck in an ocean of gray infiniteness. It made Bear Island feel tiny. It made April feel incredibly tiny. But not in the way it used to. It made her feel invincible.

"Bear?" She sat up. "Oh." The air was so sharp, bitter, and frozen that it brought on a sudden dizzy spell.

She put her head between her knees until it passed. It took a minute, maybe a bit longer. When she lifted her head again, she didn't see Bear at first.

Then she noticed him. He was sat behind her, facing the sea and staring out at it. April could sense his deep sadness.

"Bear? Oh, what is it, Bear? What's wrong?" She hurried to his side. "Why are you upset?"

She could barely look at him. Most humans were oblivious to when animals were in pain because they don't show their emotions in the same way. But April knew different. Just because you couldn't see emotion in their faces didn't mean they couldn't feel. And Bear's emotions were as real as any human's:

scudding and naked and raw.

His eyes were the worst of all. The soft melting chocolate had turned into deep, bottomless wells that April was afraid to look into lest she drown. Everything about him radiated the kind of wretchedness you would find in an empty, forlorn, forgotten graveyard or a racecourse with the tents up to hide the horse who had fallen. Bear's beautiful ears drooped so they lay flat and close to his face, and his jaw hung slack and loose. And in that moment, April realized the island's sigh had been an echo of Bear's own sadness.

"Oh, Bear."

In the end, instinct took over. She reached out and put both her arms around his neck and pressed her cheek to his fur—to the soft, fuzzy place between his ears and his eyes. And then she kissed his fur because everyone knew animal kisses were the best of all. She kissed him. And then she kissed him again and again and again. Because when she was upset, that was all she really wanted. Someone to cuddle and kiss her and make it all better.

"Something terrible must have happened to make you so sad, Bear," she whispered, her arms wrapped around his neck. "And if you're ready to tell me, I promise to listen."

19

BEAR'S STORY

IT WAS IN THIS way that Bear told April his story.

Not in words, because polar bears can't speak, but he didn't need words anyway. Sometimes all the words in the world can't *tell* a story. Instead, as April knew from experience, he told his story in the way that all animals tell their stories. It was just a matter of sitting down and listening properly. You also needed a healthy dose of instinct, sensitivity, and canny ability to fill in the gaps.

And at the top of the mountain, with the wind whirring in her ears and the cold biting at her face, she held her breath and sat and waited. At first, Bear simply paced back and forth, churning up the snow in raw, angry clumps. But after a few minutes, he positioned himself on the far edge of the summit, with his back to the island and his nose facing north.

Then it clicked.

It all clicked into place.

"Of course," she said gently. "That's the way home, isn't it? That's north."

The wind howled, somewhere in the distance waves crashed against the shore, and on the top of the mountain, April gripped hard at the truth lest it slip away.

"Directly north of here is Svalbard," she said. "That's where the ship was going. The one we came on. Tör told me a little bit about it there." She ransacked her brains to see what she could remember—very little apart from the steady blue gaze of Tör's eyes and her own seasick belly. But one thing she did recall very clearly from her conversation with Dad: "There are lots of polar bears there."

Bear slowly turned his head to face her, and in the dark brown of his eyes, she saw something she had failed to spot before. Homesickness.

"That's where you come from, isn't it?" she said softly. "That's your home."

And although he couldn't speak, there was a light that shone out of his face as he looked across toward Svalbard. It was a light as bright as the midnight sun, and she had to blink a few times to adjust.

"But Svalbard is more than two hundred miles away," she continued. "How could you have gotten all the way here? Especially if the ice caps have melted around the island?"

Bear's ears flattened against his skull. It meant he was unhappy about something. Of course he would be unhappy if the ice caps had melted. All polar bears must be. It would be like if someone came and snatched their home away from them. She crawled over to where he sat, being careful not to get too close to the edge, and rested her face against his back. He leaned into her touch, and so she stroked the place just under his ears. It was soft there. Like lullabies. And sure enough, she soon felt him relax. At the same time, her brain whirred like the machines in her father's weather cabin, trying to pull the final pieces together.

"You can't have gotten here by boat. You wouldn't have been able to swim all that way. So the only way this makes any sense is if the ice caps melted recently," she said, thinking out loud. It was true she had never actually thought to ask Dad when the ice caps around the island had melted. The encyclopedia hadn't mentioned anything about it either, so she'd just assumed it was years and years ago. Realizing it had to be a lot more recent made her chest ache in a funny way.

"I'm sorry, Bear. Human beings can be so . . . thoughtless sometimes. Okay, not me. Not even *all* humans. Most of us don't mean to, you know. We just don't know what to do about the ice caps and the plastic and the animals like you who are suffering. To be honest, it all feels so big and scary—it's like we're up against a huge wall, and so sometimes it's easier to do nothing and hope someone else will fix it." She shrugged uselessly. "Even if you want to *do* something, when you're little like me, it's so much harder to get your voice heard."

Bear growled, and it was such an unexpected noise, April fell backward.

"You're right," she said, hurriedly getting to her feet again. "That's no excuse, and you're absolutely right to be angry. Just because I'm little is no reason not to do anything. I promise I will try my hardest from now on.

Especially now that I've learned to roar."

She waited until he was settled again before sitting back down next to him.

"But I still don't understand what stopped you from getting home?"

The answer came like a sickening thud to her chest.

"Maybe you came here with your mom when you were very young, and she got sick or injured or something." April knew she was just guessing, but it was a narrative that made sense since polar bear cubs spent up to two years with their mothers. "And of course, by the time she was well enough, the ice caps around the island had already melted and so you couldn't get home."

She turned to Bear for confirmation. She had become so attuned to him that she knew exactly how to interpret his emotions, and she felt the sadness ripple out from him.

"You got stuck here." April threw her arms around

his neck and swallowed hard. The end was in sight, and she steeled herself to hear it. "And then?"

Bear lifted his head and looked out to sea for a long time. So long she didn't think he was going to finish the story. But eventually, he turned back to her, and she took a deep, shuddery breath as the truth hit her.

"Oh my. She *died*?" She racked her brains for why. "Because there wasn't enough food for both of you. Of course. Oh. Bear. That's awful." She pressed her check against his fur. She stroked his ears. She hugged him as tight as she could. She kissed the tears from his eyes. She felt her own heart skitter. "You lost your mom, and now you've been trapped on this island alone for *all* this time."

She leaned her forehead against Bear's face and reached her arms around his neck. Under her fingertips, he was trembling. "You poor, poor thing."

Bear pulled away from her and roared so hard, so

loud, so ferociously, that the earth rumbled beneath them and the clouds scurried away in fright.

"I'm going to do something about it," she vowed. "I promise."

20

TRAPPED

"WHO DO YOU REPORT the temperatures to?" April asked at breakfast the next day.

"The temperatures?" Dad looked up, startled, a cup of coffee poised in his hand. It had been a while since April had actively engaged in conversation with her father. Weeks, maybe months. Not really since the day she'd helped out in the weather cabin and he'd shouted at her. Since then she had gotten lost in her friend-ship with Bear. Not *bad* lost. *Happily* lost. The kind of lost you get in an enchanted forest where every-thing around you is edible—even the sky. But today, she looked up as if waking from a coma to realize her father was still there. She wondered, briefly, if this was how he saw her most of the time before pulling herself back to the present.

She had made a promise, after all.

"Yes. The ones you're taking," she said. "Who do you report them back to?"

He placed the cup carefully back in its saucer and looked pleased at her interest. "To the Norwegian government."

"Right." She chewed her oat biscuit deep in thought. "But what do *they* do with them?"

"It's for research, April," Dad replied. "We measure the temperatures to gauge any difference year on year."

"Yes," she said, flapping her hand. "I know *that*. But what do they actually *do* with them? Once they've got them."

"*Do?*" Dad said.

"Yes," April replied. "What are they actually doing about them? It's not just the polar bears and all the other Arctic animals it's affecting, is it? The weather in the Arctic affects *everyone* all over the planet."

"That is true." Dad looked mildly concerned, but that was about it. Then again, that was how all grown-ups looked when they talked about global warming. A spot of mild concern but nothing to worry about. The fact that the world was in crisis just didn't seem to bother them like it did April.

She bunched her fists and tried to steady her voice as she racked her brains trying to remember some of the statistics she'd read. "Ice reflects about sixty percent of the sunlight that pours down on it?"

"Eighty percent," Dad corrected.

"Eighty percent, then." She looked up at him. "So what happens when the all the ice is gone?"

"When you remove all the ice, that means the sunlight can shine straight into the ocean," Dad replied. "When that happens, the sea temperatures will rise, which in turn means the sea levels rise.'

"And the ice caps?" April asked, digging her nails into her palm to stay composed. "How much have they melted already? I know they've melted a lot . . . but how much exactly?"

Dad cleared his throat. "According to NASA, the area covered by the Arctic sea ice in summer has shrunk by over twelve percent each decade since the 1980s. Which basically equates to the loss of over one million square miles of sea ice."

"One million?!" April felt shocked, as if the floor had opened up and swallowed her whole. "So it's true? I knew they were melting, but I didn't know they were melting so fast."

"Ah," Dad said in his best teacher voice. "The polar ice caps have, in fact, melted more in the past twenty years than they did in the past ten thousand years."

"Then we have to do something!" April cried, abandoning all efforts to stay calm. "We need to reverse this somehow! Give them back their ice. Why aren't people *doing* something about it? Why aren't *you* doing more?"

Dad frowned. It was obvious he had never asked himself this question, and his bushy eyebrows knitted together like a confused caterpillar. "I don't know."

April put her oat biscuit down and brushed the crumbs off her fingers. She needed to get this conversation back on track. It wasn't Dad's fault humans had gotten the planet into this mess. It was everyone's. "You said that the ice caps are melted around Bear Island," she asked, wanting to verify Bear's story. "How fast? Is it a slow melt, or can it happen quickly?"

"Well . . . ," he said. "Normally, it's quite slow, but there was one year where there was a spike in temperatures."

"When?"

"Off the top of my head I can't remember."

"Please try!" April leaned forward and grabbed his arm. "It's really important."

Dad looked at her hand on his arm and seemed surprised to see it there. "I can check the logbooks if you are really interested."

"Can you get them now?" April urged. "Please?"

He sighed but put down his coffee, disappeared to the weather cabin, and returned with an armful of logbooks, which he placed on the counter. He opened one. "Here's the column that shows the past ten years of the annual average sea temperatures on Bear Island. You can see that the rise in temperatures is mostly steady. But here"—he jabbed his finger against one column—"the temperatures had a dramatic rise."

"The year?"

"Seven years ago."

"And you're absolutely sure this was when the last of the ice caps melted around the island?"

Dad nodded.

April sat back with a whoosh to her stomach. Bear had been here for seven years! All this time stuck on the island, unable to get home.

"But it's not fair!" she cried in frustration. "It's not *their* fault the world has ended up in this mess. It's ours!"

"It's not *whose* fault?"

April stared blankly at him.

"You said it's not *their* fault."

"The bears!" she said, exasperated. "The polar bears. The island was named after them, and they can't even come and spend their winters here anymore!"

"There is a cruel irony to that. And . . . of course it is terribly sad," he added hurriedly.

"And the ice caps?" she persisted. "The ones closer to the North Pole. The ones around Svalbard. They're still there, aren't they?"

"Yes," he said. "For the time being."

"So polar bears can still live there?" she asked.

He nodded.

Looking at Dad with marmalade caught on his

whiskers, his thin, papery fingers, and his crooked nose buried in those logbooks, she thought he wasn't an obvious savior. But he was the only one she had. She crossed her fingers for luck and then gave him her best smile. It might have come out as a grimace, but never mind. "What if I told you there was a bear stuck on the island all this time?"

He didn't even look up.

"Dad!" April said more firmly. "There's a polar bear on the island, and I need your help."

"Hmm?" He glanced distractedly at her, and she could tell he was only half listening.

"Listen to me, please?" She was struggling to contain her voice, and it kept coming out wobbly. "There *is* a polar bear here. And he's the kindest, bestest bear in the whole wide world. And I need your help, so please can you drop that logbook RIGHT NOW?"

Dad did indeed drop the logbook, and it fell to the floor with a loud rustle. She had his full attention. But not in the way she wanted. In fact, he was looking at her in a way that made her stomach squirm.

"April," he said very slowly and carefully. "What did you say?"

April gulped. "There's a polar bear on the island."

Dad stared at her a long time before answering. "There. Are. No. Bears. Left. On. Bear. Island," he said, shaking his head. "It's simply impossible."

"But there is one! And he's not at all dangerous," she cried. "I just want to help him, don't you see? This isn't where he should be!"

Dad continued to stare at her as if she had lost her mind and then, worst of all, seemed to think she was joking and began to pick up his logbook.

"You don't believe me, do you? Well, go check the storeroom!" she said recklessly. "You'll know I'm telling the truth then!"

"The storeroom? What has that got to do with anything?"

"You'll see. Just check it!"

He rose slowly to his feet, and clearing his throat a couple of times, he opened the storeroom door. "APRIL!" He grabbed the doorframe for support. "The food! Where has it all gone?"

"I just told you! He was starving—all skin and bones. But because he's hunting again plus all the food I've been feeding him, you should see him now. He looks—"

Dad swiveled around to face her. "April, what have you done?"

It was a tone of voice she had never heard before, and she swallowed hard.

"I gave it to Bear."

"To Bear."

She nodded.

"To a polar bear."

Dad sat down on the sofa with a thump. The log-books were scattered around his feet, and he had an odd, faraway expression on his face that made April feel hot and clammy. "Granny Apples was right," he said. "It *was* a mistake to bring you here. The sailors said the island could do funny things to the mind. All this time alone and it's my fault. For working so hard and not spending as much time with you as I would have liked. Why, it's only natural you would create an imaginary friend to keep you company."

"He's not an imaginary friend!" she yelled. "I'm like Mom. I'm just different. You even said it yourself!"

"Yes, but the difference is she didn't make up animals, April, and then throw all our food away." His gray eyes narrowed with a kind of horrible, cloying pity that made her want to sob in frustration. "My dear child, is this about you wanting attention?"

"No," she said, turning her head so he wouldn't see her tears. "I've given up on that a long time ago."

Dad chose that exact moment to blow his nose loudly into his handkerchief. "Right, then," he declared once he'd finished, utterly oblivious to what she'd said. "It's just as well we only have six weeks left on the island."

"Six weeks?" April gasped. "We only have six weeks left?"

21

THE PLAN

IN THE DAYS that followed, April would catch Dad's gaze upon her. Not a warm, cozy, fatherly gaze. But a narrow-eyed, distrustful one that made her feel like a stranger every time she was in his company. He even counted every single food item left in the storeroom so it would be impossible to take any more—although luckily she had already foreseen this emergency and had an extra stash under her bed. But it wasn't nearly enough to last six weeks, and it now felt more urgent than ever to come up with a plan to help Bear.

"How did we get so messy?" April gazed around the living room as if seeing it for the first time. She had been so busy all summer having fun that the pile of unwashed clothes, cups, teapots, and empty cans of soup had somehow passed her by. But in the end, she found the book on the Arctic Circle sandwiched between a jar of stale coffee and one of Dad's paisley vests and quickly found the section on Svalbard. A couple of aniseed candy wrappers fell out. It turned out to be an archipelago of islands about halfway between Norway and the North Pole, with about 60 percent of it made up of glaciers. It was home to seabirds, arctic foxes, reindeer, and about three thousand polar bears.

"I've got it!"

A surge of something hot coursed through her veins as the answer finally came. It was obvious! So obvious it had been staring her in the face the whole time. There was only one thing to do. She didn't have to leave Bear in his horrible lonely cave.

She would take him home.

Home to Svalbard.

"You'll have lots of friends there. Maybe some relatives too! Like cousins and aunts and uncles. Perhaps even a mate," she whispered, hoping that Bear could hear her across the island. "You won't be alone anymore."

The only problem was the distance.

Svalbard was about a day's boat ride from Bear Island. Much too far for Bear to swim by himself, otherwise he would have returned home a long time ago. Yet there had to be another way of getting him there—even without Dad's help.

And she had the beginnings of a plan.

★

The upturned boat on Walrus Bay wasn't really a boat at all.

"More of a canoe," April mused as she stood before it. "But a big canoe. Big enough for the pair of us, anyway."

It had a yellow painted hull and curved upward at

either end like a Viking ship. In places, the paint was peeling off, but when April rubbed the boat with her mitten, it still managed to shine a little bit like a winter sun.

"Once upon a time, you were very pretty, weren't you? I wonder how you ended up here. Did you get left behind too?" She gazed around at the remnants of all the things the humans had left behind in Walrus Bay. The dilapidated hut, the ruined jetty, the rusted cable, and a couple of freshly washed-up plastic bottles. "How did we get so messy?" she asked for the second time that day.

She sighed and turned her focus back to the boat. Inside were two wooden benches, an old oar, and plenty of pebbles, sand, shells, and dirt. But luckily, no sign of any holes.

"The first thing is to clean you out."

Out of the corner of her eye, she saw the sea crashing against the shore. Some of the waves were as tall as she was. Most were taller. April's stomach jittered and jumped. Fox poop. But no matter how dangerous the journey would be and no matter how sick she got on the boat, she was determined to get Bear home.

The alternative was unthinkable.

The next couple of days were spent poring over maps and the all-essential survival tips for a long boat journey as detailed by the encyclopedia. However, the more she read up on sailing, the more underprepared she felt. Who knew that the shape of the waves could foretell a shift in the wind, or that the particular words used in sailing terminology were almost as big as a dictionary, or that you needed to have a sixth sense about the weather conditions?

April faced the map of Bear Island on the wall and chewed her lip anxiously. There was only one thing to do. This was most definitely an emergency, and since Dad was in the weather cabin, now was the perfect moment.

She'd kept the envelope in her bedside drawer. It smelled faintly of mackerel, old rope, and something else. It was a comforting, safe smell, and that was what finally persuaded her to dial the number before she could talk herself out of it.

The phone rang twice. *"Hallo?"* The line was surprisingly clear, as if he were only in the next room. *"Hallo?"*

Her mouth had gone inexplicably dry. "Tör?" she managed to croak at last. "It's me. April. April Wood."

"April?" he said, sounding surprised, as if he had never actually expected to hear from her ever again. "Is everything all right on the island?"

She nodded and then realized he couldn't see her. "Yes," she replied hurriedly. "It's all fine."

April paused. She'd never been good on the telephone at the best of times, and speaking to someone she'd only met once just made her even more nervous. She gripped the phone tighter.

"How can I help you?" he said into the silence.

"I just wanted to ask you a question about sailing," she said, crossing her fingers and hoping she sounded believable. "I'm. . . writing up a report for school, and I need to show people how to get from Bear Island to Svalbard by boat."

"And you want to make sure the boat goes in the right direction?" he asked. "So the people don't end up in New York?"

"Something like that," she admitted.

"Well, in the olden days, we used the map of the sky to find our way."

"The map of the sky?" The encyclopedia hadn't mentioned that. "You mean the stars?"

"That's right. But these days a compass is much handier."

Phew. She had one of those.

"You would also need a chart of the Barents Sea."

She looked at the map. Slightly old and dog-eared.

But it would have to do.

"And a GPS."

"A what?"

"It's connected to the satellite and shows your positioning." Tör said just as the phone began to hiss. He spoke louder to make himself heard. "Everywhere in the world, even tiny little places like Bear Island, has a set of coordinates. Sailors use them as a navigational tool. We think of them as modern-day stars."

"But can you do it without a GPS?" she asked, raising her own voice. "Or the stars?"

"Yes," he said just as the phone began to crackle and break up. He spoke louder over the hiss. "But . . . harder . . . rely . . . your compass. Set it . . . the coordinates . . . Svalbard. Be . . . careful . . . winds."

She could get the coordinates from the map—that was easy enough to do—and then follow the compass all the way there.

"April?" he asked as the line suddenly became clear

again. "Are you still there?"

"Oh!" With a start, she noticed Dad outside the window and headed directly toward the cabin. "I have to go," she said quickly. "But thank you!"

And before Tör had time to take another breath, let alone answer, she hung up.

"Everything all right, April?" asked Dad as he entered the cabin with a blast of frosty air and a hint of aniseed candy.

"Absolutely fine," she said, passing him on her way out.

There was nothing else to lose. It was time to tell Bear.

★

When she reached Walrus Bay, he was playing in the waves—ducking under them like a seal and emerging moments later with a beam of happiness. He hadn't seen her yet, and so she watched him.

She couldn't help compare what she was seeing now

to what she had seen when they first met. His coat was no longer gray and matted and rough. It was now sleek and shiny, and it glistened like stardust. His ears had stopped drooping. Instead, they danced on his head and twitched with life. She could no longer count all his ribs. In fact, he had filled out and perhaps even gotten slightly plump. His face wore the contented glow of someone who had just eaten their favorite dinner and was about to do a large burp.

He looked how all polar bears should look.

Happy. Healthy. Hearty.

With a choke, she suddenly realized their time was coming to a close. Only a week ago, the sun had finally disappeared over the horizon, marking the end of the midnight sun for another year. Even her watch had started working again, ticktocking down their days together.

"Bear," she whispered, her voice cracking like sandpaper.

He heard her then. His head lifted, his ears twitched, and his whole face lit up. The way it always lit up when he saw April. Shaking the water from his coat so it sprayed in thousands of rainbow droplets all over the beach, he bounded over in a gallop. When he reached her side, he gently nuzzled her shoulder in greeting and then licked her face a couple of times too. Once they had both roared at each other, he rested his chin against her chest and breathed in her scent.

It was a scent that felt like home.

April blinked a few times, buried her nose into his fur, wrapped her arms around him, and swallowed hard. She didn't even need to say anything.

Bear knew.

Her throat felt thick, and she gazed hard at the snowcapped mountains before trusting herself to speak. "I have to go home soon," she managed to say at last. "Not because I want to. But because I *have* to. I have to go to school so I can pass some exams, which means I'll have the paperwork to do something important when I grow up," she said. "But you know what? I don't even have to wait till I'm grown up. I can't leave it to other people to fix anymore. I'm going to *do* something to help save the Arctic—and maybe even the planet. And that something starts right now." She took a deep breath. "I'm not leaving you, Bear. I've got a plan."

She squared his face in her hands so they were looking at each other eye to eye. His eyes were chocolate and warm and shiny. They gazed at her in a way that made her insides melt. She didn't think she'd ever find anyone in her whole life who would look at her the way Bear did in that moment.

"It's a dangerous plan, but we don't have much of a choice. It's either that or . . . well, *that's* not going to happen. Hush. It's okay." She wiped the dampness from his face with her fingertips and scratched the place that he loved under his left ear. "The truth is, I'm scared. I'm not nearly as brave as you. I could never have been here alone all those years like you have. But it's better than doing nothing, and as you know, human beings are very good at doing nothing. I don't want to be that kind of person anymore." She lifted her chin and spoke more confidently than she felt. "So you have to promise to come with me even if you think it's the worst idea in the world."

That's when April pointed to the boat.

Bear's ears twitched, his whiskers rattled, and he backed away so suddenly, she was forced to let go lest she be thrown across the beach. He immediately rose up on his rear legs, towering above her like a sky-scraper, and roared in rage. It was by far the loudest roar she had ever heard him make, and if they had been standing on the cliff edge, then it probably would have traveled to the moon and back at least a few times.

Once he had finished, she took her fingers out of her ears and lifted herself to her full April-sized height.

"Here's the thing, Bear. I'm going to do it whether you like it or not," she said. "You can't stop me. But it would be a whole lot easier if you did agree. . . ."

Bear roared again, deafening out the rest of what she was about to say. And this time even the sun hid, the earth trembled, and the mountain quavered. He roared and raved and ranted for what felt like a very long time—although it was hard to tell exactly how long. But long enough for April to sit down by the upturned boat, play cat's cradle at least ten times, and have a quick nap. In the end, Bear just roared himself out, as she knew he would.

"This is your only choice. You can't stay here," she whispered. He eventually rested his chin on her shoulder, moaned softly, and then licked her face. "I'm taking you home."

22

AN UNWANTED SURPRISE

APRIL RETURNED TO Walrus Bay every day for the next week. And every day she thanked all the trillions of stars in the northern sky that Dad was having difficulties with one of his key instruments—because the time spent trying to repair it meant he failed to notice what she was up to behind his back.

The biggest challenge was food. Even with tight rationing, the stash under her bed was almost all gone, so she had to race and make sure the boat would be ready before the food ran out. But she also needed to save some food for the journey.

So far, she had stocked the boat with:

- three jars of crunchy peanut butter (leaving just one under her bed);
- the last four packs of oat biscuits;
- one can of tomato soup for herself and three cans of meaty stew for Bear;
- one can of peaches in syrup (she wasn't a fan, but Bear had pleaded with his best melting eyes to bring some sugary treats);
- three of Dad's aniseed candies (this was more for sentimental reasons—even though they'd had a fight, she still wanted something to remind her of him);
- two gallons of water;
- a can opener;
- Dad's Swiss Army knife;
- the compass to direct them to Svalbard;
- the book on the Arctic Circle, which included a rough map of the Barents Sea between Bear Island and Svalbard;

- a tarpaulin to protect the boat from tall waves and storms;
- some seasickness tablets;
- her waterproof trousers and jacket, plus a waterproof hat;
- two pairs of woolly socks;
- the sweater Granny Apples knitted for her at Christmas the year before last, even though it was a bit short in the arms now;
- a ziplock bag she'd found in the kitchen cupboard;
- the cabin's first-aid kit (she had a pang about taking this because what if Dad hurt himself?);
- her pillow;
- and, finally, her heart-shaped pebble.

Some of the items, like the water, were so heavy that she had to enlist Bear to help her drag the sled. But the others she managed to squirrel away easily in her backpack. Unfortunately, what she didn't have, and perhaps needed most of all, was a life jacket. But she would take the satellite phone instead. It would be essential for emergencies, although it did worry her to leave Dad without it.

The operation to fix the boat was harder.

First, she had to persuade Bear to tip it over the right way up, and next she had to repair it. Luckily there was a book in the cabin all about boats, and using this guidance combined with memories of the fishermen on the docks preparing their boats at the start of summer, she cleared all the debris from the inside, and using the sandpaper she found in the storeroom, she smoothed down all the nicks, the ticks, and the bumpy bits. This was much tougher than it looked. Day after day, she returned to Walrus Bay until her arms ached, her fingers were scratched red raw, and her lower back throbbed.

In the weather cabin, she'd found some nails and

a hammer, and using one of the loose planks from the deserted cabin, she created a small partition in the base of the boat so their belongings wouldn't slide around everywhere. She also repaired the seat with a soft piece of driftwood. Once the boat was loaded, the final job was to nail on the tarpaulin so it would protect them from tall waves, bad weather, and maybe even walruses. There were many worries that kept her awake at night, but the biggest one was how to make sure the boat would find its way north to Svalbard, let alone how she would find her way back home again afterward. She had the compass, but with no engine or sail, she was reliant on one oar, which she'd have to row herself.

It was a big ask. But since she didn't have any alternative other than leaving Bear here, it would have to do.

★

The date for departure was set for September 10, which was the absolute longest she could stretch out their provisions.

"There's hardly any food left," April told Bear. "So we have to leave on that date. Don't worry—it's still a week away, and hopefully the weather might be nicer by then."

Since she'd finished the boat, the island had been deluged by rain. Not the kind of fine drizzle April had gotten used to back home, but thick, heavy, fat rain that sliced through the air like needles. Rain that swept across the island in sheets and made the waves rear up like alligators.

Rain that also chilled April to the bone every time she went out and eventually gave her a nasty cold, some loud sneezes, and a very runny nose.

She'd been resting on the sofa in front of the fire for the past two days. She'd rather have been in bed so she could keep away from Dad's gaze; every so often she'd catch him staring at her. But it was cold in her bedroom. Her head throbbed. Her skin felt damp with sweat. Her tongue felt thick. Even if she'd wanted to move, she couldn't. She was armed with a box of tissues, some watery tomato soup, and feeling decidedly sorry for herself as well as worrying about Bear.

"Good news," said Dad, putting down the satellite phone.

"Hmmm?" April snuffled.

Dad had used the satellite phone earlier today to find out how to fix an instrument that wasn't working. This call, April assumed, was the engineer calling him back.

"That was my boss, Mr. Olsen," Dad said. "The guy who is taking over from us is arriving sooner than expected."

"What?" She sneezed violently. "Why?"

"Apparently his previous placement finished earlier than anticipated, and he's happy to start early," he continued. "Means we can go home, April. I don't know about you, but I think I'm ready for some creature comforts again. And just imagine! Marmalade on warm, buttery toast. Freshly baked scones dribbled with raspberry jam. And ground coffee with fresh milk."

"But . . ." Her throat felt tight and constricted. Her heart hammered. She tried to speak, but the words jammed in her throat. "But . . ."

Scones? Marmalade? Ground coffee?

"We can't leave yet!"

"But you'll be better off there," Dad said, throwing her another of those looks. "Don't you want to go home?"

"No!" she cried, and sneezed once more. "I need more time."

"Time for what?"

"You gave me this watch at the beginning of summer and said it was because of *friluftsliv*. Now you're just taking the *friluftsliv* away!"

Dad opened and closed his mouth. April knew she wasn't being particularly clear, but she didn't know how to explain herself. How could she? Her head was full of cold, and her brain felt scrambled. She couldn't bring up Bear again, not after their last conversation had ended so badly. But all she could picture was his face and the pleading look in his eyes whenever he gazed at her.

In the end, she started crying. Not big ugly sobs, but tiny tears of frustration that trickled out against her will and ran down her cheeks. She rubbed them away furiously. "You always take everything away I love."

Dad looked startled, as if she had thrown a glass of ice-cold water all over him. "That's not true."

"It is true!" she cried. "You took away the rat I rescued!"

"That's because it was a rat," he said, pulling his hankie out of his jacket pocket and shaking it clear of aniseed candy wrappers before offering it to her. "It didn't belong in the house."

"What about the animal rescue center?"

"What animal rescue center?"

"Exactly!" She blew her nose. "They want volunteers to help muck out the horses, but I need a permission slip to work there. I've asked you so many times, but you still haven't signed it!"

"But . . . how can there be horses in the middle of the city?" he asked, tentatively taking back the snotty hankie. "I didn't even realize there was a stable nearby."

"That's because you never listen to me!" April yelled in exasperation. "You don't know anything about what I want! You said we were coming to the Arctic Circle to spend time together. But you lied! You're so busy being sad over Mom the whole time, you don't even see me! Either that, or you're working!"

Dad's eyebrows did that funny darting thing they did whenever he was nervous. His mouth curled at the edges, and he cleared his throat. "Maybe we can . . . arrange horseback-riding lessons when we go home."

"I DON'T WANT HORSE-RIDING LESSONS!"

April didn't mean to roar. It just came out. If Bear were here, he would be proud of her, because it was the loudest roar she'd done so far. The force of it was so earsplitting that Dad's hand jerked and the coffee in his cup splashed upward into his face. After he had mopped his brow with the snotty hankie and taken a steadying breath, he opened his eyes wide and looked at April as if he was seeing her for the first time in years.

April stared back.

The roar was subsiding in her chest, but her heart still thumped furiously and the blood pumped around her veins like hot molten lava.

"I don't even care about that anymore," she repeated in a still, level voice. "I'm just not ready to go home yet."

"April?" Dad stretched out his hand as if he were going to pat her shoulder but then had second thoughts and retracted it. "The thing is I wasn't going to agree but . . . after that conversation about the polar bear and then the situation with the food . . . I thought . . . I thought you would be better off back home. So . . . I said yes."

"Say un-yes, then!"

"It's too late," Dad said. "He'll be here tomorrow."

NO MORE TIME

APRIL LIKED TO THINK that she was more grown-up than other girls her age. "I might be short, but at least I'm not a crybaby," she would often say to herself.

But tonight she stormed off into her bedroom, slammed the door, threw herself facedown on the bed, and screamed into her pillow. Dad knocked once, knocked again, but then left her alone. After a bit, Mozart's Concerto for Flute and Harp filled the cabin. It was a peaceful, soothing piece, and breath by breath, April started to feel calmer again.

It was the shock, that was all.

She hadn't meant to shout and roar at Dad. The look on his face! Had she ever seen him so frightened? No. Not since the time he'd caught her doing cartwheels on their shed roof and gone sheet white. She giggled despite herself but then stopped, and the giggle ran out of her like curdled milk.

The new meteorologist was coming tomorrow.

Tomorrow!

Already she could hear Dad starting to pack up his belongings. She sat up purposefully and shook her head to get rid of the cold. First, she tilted her head to the left so it could drain out through her ear. Then she tilted it to the right to get rid of the straggly bits. When her head finally felt less foggy, she snapped open the window, and a rush of cold, stark air blew in and barked in her face.

At long last, her head started to clear.

The island was bathed in weak evening sun, and although the rain had stopped, there was still water hovering in the air. She would never see this view again. Never see the way the sun made the sea look pink. Never see how the sky looked like apricots. Never see the trio of snowcapped mountains marking the horizon, the wild gorse, the hundreds of blue lakes, or any more of the secret places she'd explored over the past few months.

She gazed hard and long and drank it all in until she was giddy.

There was no sign of Bear.

It didn't matter. She knew he would hear her anyway.

"It's tonight," she whispered, cupping her hands around her mouth. "I'll meet you by the boat at midnight."

She pricked her ears in the way Bear had taught her to listen. She heard the distant thunder of the waves, gulls screeching, the sigh of the mountains, and the gentle exhale of the earth.

And then.

There it was.

Bear's roar.

The tremor of it bounced and ricocheted and zipped over the earth and finally reached her window and thudded against her heart. She held his roar close to her chest, sank back onto her bed, and breathed it into herself from top to toe. After a while, she no longer noticed her aches and pains or her snotty nose. She felt filled with something far more powerful.

She was filled with Bear energy.

The boat was ready.

And now she had to be ready too.

★

She waited until about eleven, pulled on her rainbow boots, and tugged her warmest hat down low. There was just one last thing to do.

In a saucepan, she quietly heated some of the UHT

milk, stirred in the chocolate, and then wrote Dad a short goodbye note. She had deliberated over the words all evening.

> Dear Dad,
>
> I'm sorry I shouted at you earlier today. I didn't mean it. I was just worried about Bear and I AM telling the truth.
>
> I love you.
>
> April
>
> P.S. Please don't follow because it will be too dangerous.

She couldn't remember the last time she had told Dad she loved him. Not since Mom was alive. It felt a bit silly thinking about that now. Just because Mom was gone didn't mean they couldn't love each other.

Even though they had fought and the summer

hadn't gone quite according to plan, the thought of his thatch of salt-and-pepper hair, wild eyebrows, and gentle gray eyes almost stopped her. How odd that on the point of leaving, she could suddenly think of a billion and one things to say to him:

- Thank you for the daily boxes of chocolates when she'd had chicken pox that time and had to take three weeks off school.
- That her favorite Mozart tune was "Voi che sapete" from *The Marriage of Figaro* because it made her feel like dancing.
- How he should buy himself some rainbow boots because it would make him seem less serious.
- That she regretted not asking him more about his work at the university and whether he actually enjoyed it or not.
- And what his favorite memory of Mom was so maybe they could share it together.

But it was too late for all of that.

So she left the teapot, his mug, and the note outside his bedroom door, and without stopping to think about it too much, she pushed her backpack through the bedroom window and then, with a small grunt of effort, followed it herself.

24

THE BOAT

THE RAIN RETURNED and drove down in thick, heavy curtains all the way to Walrus Bay. It trickled down the back of April's neck, ran down her spine, and even managed to get inside her boots.

By the time she made it to the boat, she realized she had forgotten the satellite phone. She couldn't risk going back to get it, and she kicked herself for being so forgetful. When she saw Bear, she rested her face against his chest. It was like enveloping herself in the softest fleece, or wearing a hundred fluffy cats, or being cuddled by a giant hot water bottle. After a few minutes, her teeth stopped chattering.

Close up, he smelled the way all animals smell. Slightly feral, musky, but sweet at the same time. It felt safe and comforting. They stayed like that long after they both needed to. But then, bear hugs are the best, so it didn't really matter how long it was.

"I suppose we'd better go."

The boat was too heavy for April, so she had to rely on Bear to move it for her. But getting Bear to understand was a different matter, since he was far more interested in playing with the waves. In the end, she put her own shoulder to the hull and desperately tried to push, but it was no use. She might as well have been trying to move a mountain. With the rain lashing down, she banged her palms against the boat in frustration.

It was then Bear came over in curiosity, lowered his shoulders, and shoved the boat. Mischievously at first, as if it were a game, and then gradually with more and more strength.

April fell back in relief, her breath ragged in her chest.

"Come on, Bear! You can do it!"

But still the boat didn't budge one inch. What if it had gotten jammed? What if it was too heavy? What if Bear was stuck here forever?

She held her breath.

Bear pushed harder. He pushed with all the force and magnitude of the bear he was. He roared and grunted and heaved. The boat finally started to creak from side to side, but still it didn't move. It shuddered, creaked, and groaned. The noise was like nails and dentists' drills.

Bear bared his teeth and lowered his head. Going for one more powerful, brute-force push. And then the boat made a scraping noise. Then another.

"It's moving! You're doing it!"

Inch by inch, the boat crept closer and closer to the shore's edge until the first wave splashed over the hull. April, who had been cheering every single inch of progress, took the opportunity to jump into the boat. She gasped and spluttered in shock as the seawater landed on her like ice-cold rain.

"Just one more push, Bear, and we'll be in the water!"

Bear sank his shoulders and drew on every ounce of strength he had. Then, with one last, mighty shove, the boat left Walrus Bay and finally bobbed up and down on the sea.

"We're afloat!" she yelled as the boat climbed the first wave and then dropped back down.

Bear stood on the shore watching, and for a horrible, heart-sickening moment, April thought he wasn't going to join her, and she'd be left to drift off all by herself. She put her fingers in her mouth and whistled, praying he would get the message. Luckily, he didn't need asking twice. Bear leaped into the water and started to swim toward her.

By the time he arrived and had climbed aboard, tipping the boat precariously this way and that, April hugged him fiercely. When she let go, she was soggy, and the boat was already far out to sea, rocking and rolling on the cold gray waves.

As she battled to secure the tarpaulin, she remembered her father's warning not to go too close to the shore's edge. It was too late now. Bear Island had disappeared from sight. Her stomach flip-flopped, and she hurriedly tied the last knot in place.

"We're on our way," she whispered, cuddling up to Bear in the darkness and crossing her fingers for luck. "Next stop Svalbard."

★

She didn't know how many hours had passed, but enough time for her to do some rowing, which was much harder than she had ever imagined, eat some cold soup, share the chocolate cookies, and somehow have a nap, curled up against Bear in the bottom of the boat. When she woke, it was because they were on a roller coaster. Up they soared. High, high as a kite. At the top, her tummy did that funny squeezy thing. Then down, down they plummeted.

April flung out her arms to protect herself. But there wasn't much to grip onto. In the end, she clung to the seat. The wood bit into her palms, and her toes were numb with cold. The boat lurched again. Her tummy somersaulted. Her chin jarred against her chest.

In front of her, Bear whimpered.

"Shhh, don't be afraid now," she murmured, letting go of the seat to touch his cheek. "We'll be fine. See? The compass is still facing north."

The boat soared again, like a plane lifting itself from the runway. They soared higher, hit the top of the wave, and plummeted back down, and April bit back her scream.

"It's okay," she said as Bear whimpered again. "We'll

be fine. I'll just take a quick look outside to see if we're nearly there yet."

Her fingers were icy raw, and she struggled to untie the rope that secured the tarpaulin. She gnawed at it with her teeth until it loosened and then peeked through the gap.

"Oh my."

As far as she could see, there was nothing but writhing gray waves surrounding the boat from all angles. But not the kind of waves that had hit the shore back on Bear Island. These waves were monstrous. Colossal in size. Rearing up like trees. So grotesquely large they made the boat look like a miniature toy.

April swallowed.

There was no land.

There was no anything—except the horrible, hideous waves and them.

Bear sat huddled at the far end of the boat and

stared at her with huge chocolate eyes. She reached out her fingers and stroked him under his ear.

"It's all fine." She closed the tarpaulin with a snap and decided not to mention the black clouds to him.

25

THE STORM

THE STORM STARTED with a crack of thunder and the jarring, frantic drumming of rain on the tarpaulin. It was like camping—hiding inside the tent while the rain fell. Except in a tent you felt safe and cozy and protected.

April felt none of those things.

The waves had grown more monstrous.

She didn't have to peek out from under the tarpaulin to know this, because every time the boat climbed, it seemed to reach higher and higher. Surely it couldn't get much worse?

But it did.

The boat soared so high, it was as if they were climbing a ladder into space. They would perch precariously at the top of the wave, sway from side to side, and then plunge back down into the abyss.

April had long since stopped trying to smother her screams.

It didn't matter anymore. Bear's eyes were wide with panic, and the smell inside the boat had become tight and fearful. All the time, the rain beat down, the waves crashed, and the thunder bellowed. She crawled to the middle and put her arms around Bear. Their faces touched, and his breath was hot on her face.

"I'm sorry," she whispered. "This is all my fault."

Bear touched her nose with his own. Under her hands, his heart beat. Her own chest thudded and scuttered.

"I love you." She pressed her lips against his face and kissed him. "I love you *so* much."

She nestled closer to him, and somewhere in the bowels of her being, she knew he loved her back. For a sweet, perfect moment, everything was safe.

And then the wave came.

It seemed to rear up from the very depths of the ocean, and with callous cruelty, it tossed them high into the heavens. The boat spiraled and danced in the gray sky, hovering in midair before falling hard. It smacked onto the waves with a loud crash and flipped upside down.

April screamed.

Bear roared.

As the boat smashed violently into the water, the tarpaulin was ripped clean off, the oar got sucked away, and the bow end snapped in two. The water was so icy she gasped. And as she gasped, the water filled her mouth. She panicked and flailed out her hands to try to reach Bear, but she got pulled underwater, and her hands just stretched into a frozen nothingness.

The water was pummeling her everywhere. She was flung upside down, tossed on her side, and then hurled onto her back. Her rainbow boots were torn off, and the sheer shock of the water on her skin made her cry.

It didn't matter that she swallowed more water, that it tasted like rancid salt, or that the temperature was slowly freezing her organs one by one. It didn't even matter that the boat had fallen apart and all her belongings were now sinking to the bottom of the sea. None of that would matter if she had Bear.

And finally, just when she thought she wouldn't be able to hold her breath anymore, the currents pushed her back up to the surface, and there he was. She could just about see him. But he was so far away from her. Too far! She stretched out her hands again.

"BEAR!"

Bear's mouth opened in a roar. She could see it, but

she couldn't hear it. But he was there—swimming frantically toward her. His ears pinned back. And a fierce, protective expression on his face.

Her fingertips touched his paw. So nearly there! So nearly safe.

But the sea hadn't finished with her yet. The current twisted its finger around her ankles, tore her from his grasp, and sucked her back under.

She fought. Her legs and arms thrashed. She screamed.

But it was so cold.

So very, very cold.

And the sea just kept on pulling. It kept sucking, yanking, and dragging her deeper and deeper. Into the murky depths where not even the midnight sun ventured. Where the water was heavy and dark and deathly. Where no eleven-year-old girl belonged.

There, the water settled around her like frost.

And eventually, after a long, hard battle, April closed her eyes.

It was just so bitterly cold.

And then it all . . .

went . . .

black.

WHERE'S BEAR?

"APRIL?" The voice was distant—coming to her from a faraway land. "April?"

She was lying on a bunk in a cabin that smelled of mackerel. Standing over her was . . .

"*Dad?*"

"April!" His face crumpled, and he leaned forward and pulled her into a hug. He smelled of aniseed and tweed but also of hot chocolate and home. "My girl."

When he finally let go, he seemed shocked by his own emotion. As he dabbed his eyes, April struggled to think.

Because lots of things didn't make sense.

Why did her head feel full of icebergs?

How come she was back in this cabin? It was the same cargo ship, wasn't it? The one they had arrived on all those months ago.

Was her dad *crying*?

And something else.

Something she couldn't put her finger on. But nevertheless something very important. Something she simply must remember.

But then the pain in her head came back, like piercing shards of ice, and she slipped into the black once more.

★

When she woke up the second time, she thought at first the cabin was empty. There was nothing but the sound of her own raspy breathing and some dreams she couldn't remember.

The voice startled her. He was sitting on a chair on the other side of the room folding his handkerchief into small, meticulous squares. "What were you doing out there?"

April tried to answer, but the ice in her head was rattling around. Because what *was* she doing out there?

"You could have been killed!" Dad sprang up from his chair and strode toward the bed, staring down at April with such a raw, naked gaze she wanted to shrink back into the pillow. She hadn't seen this level of emotion on his face since her mother's funeral, and it unnerved her to think she had put it there.

"I know," she said finally, and even though every bone in her body ached, she rested her hand on his arm. "I'm so sorry."

He took a shaky breath, sat down on the edge of the bed, and slowly replaced the hankie in his pocket. Then he did something he hadn't done for a very long time; he placed his own hand on top of hers. For a moment, neither of them spoke. But sometimes you don't need to say words for what's in your heart.

"The last thing I remember was falling under the water," April said, choosing her words carefully. "But after that . . . it's all black."

She tried hard to remember what had happened, but it was like coming up against a deep, murky fog, and the harder she tried, the more her head hurt.

"By the time I had realized you were gone," Dad said, "it was morning and the ship had arrived with the new meteorologist and his assistant. We looked everywhere and . . ." He cleared his throat a couple of times, and April laced her fingers into his. "And then we saw the trail marks on the beach and realized you had taken the boat. The captain didn't think it possible—because how could a little girl push a boat like that out to sea? But that boy, Tör, he was the one who guessed where you might have headed."

"Oh!" April exclaimed.

There was a rushing in her ears, the sound of

waterfalls and something else. Something loud and visceral and raw.

"Bear!" She sat bolt upright with a start, blood shooting through her veins like volcanoes. "Where is he?!"

Dad opened and closed his mouth and turned a peculiar shade of red.

"No!" She pushed the covers off her, rushed unsteadily past Dad, yanked open the door, and ran out onto the deck barefoot.

"April!"

The wind smacked her in the face, and the deck smelled grimy and dirty. A couple of crew members hovered nearby and looked at her curiously.

"Where is he?" she shouted, staring around her frantically. "WHERE IS BEAR?"

The wind howled, the engine throbbed, and every cell in her body ached. Around her, gulls screamed and dipped in the endless arching sky. She ran the entire length of the deck, the cold snapping and snarling at her skin. There was nothing but coiled-up rope, oil, and the bitter Arctic air on her face. She leaned over the edge and stared as hard as she could at the horizon in all directions, but the only thing she could see was stark empty seas.

"Bear!"

She sank back away from the railing, her face numb, her fingers frozen, and she stumbled into the nearest doorway. The heavy metal door swung shut behind her, and she was suddenly in the dark, closed passageway that twisted and turned in the bowels of the ship. It wouldn't do to panic. She took a deep breath and calmed herself down. Now she could hear. Listen—as Bear had taught her to do. Her ears pricked. Her senses on full alert. At first, she heard nothing over the loud throb of the ship's engines, but then . . . there was something. So small she almost missed it. She tuned in to the noise, and with a beating, dancing heart, she followed the passageway all the way down to the murky underbelly of the hold. Here she came face-to-face with another closed metal door—this one being guarded by Tör.

"Hello," he said.

Apart from a brief glance his way, she barely noticed him. Her whole body tingled with fear and antici-pation. Tör took a large key from his pocket, slowly swung the door, and then stood back.

On the far side of the room, crouched low on the floor and with a metal chain tied tightly around his neck, was Bear.

27

COURAGE

"BEAR!"

April forgot that her body ached, her head throbbed, and she was lucky to be alive. Seeing Bear made her forget everything—even her own pain.

She raced to his side, dropping to her knees in a huge whoosh, and threw her arms around his neck. Like an excitable puppy, he whimpered and squirmed and licked her face. His bright chocolate eyes drank her in and made her tummy all gooey. She buried her face in his soft, downy fur, and they clung together.

When she finally pulled back, Bear licked her face and growled gently. Not an angry growl. But a happy growl. A growl of deep contentment. She cupped his cheeks in her hands and kissed his nose.

"When you called me to ask me how to get to Svalbard, I thought it was strange." She had forgotten Tör was behind her. "Of all the crazy questions to ask. But even crazier to take a boat and actually try to do it."

"I have to thank you, then," April said, placing her cheek against Bear's. "Because you knew where to find us."

Tör stared at the pair of them, as if trying to compute something that didn't make sense. "You were in his mouth when we found you. He was treading water, and there you were just hanging out of his jaws. We thought he was trying to kill you."

She could still feel the icy-cold water deep inside her body and the horrible sensation of falling somewhere deep and dark and bottomless. She shuddered and gulped and shivered all over.

"He saved me, didn't he?" April said, her throat

thickening. "Bear saved my life."

She hugged Bear tight, knowing that no words could ever be enough. But even without words, she knew he would understand.

When April finally let go, she gazed hard at Tör. "Don't tell me. I suppose you tried to kill him?"

"My father," Tör explained, lifting up his palms in apology. "He is different from us. You have to understand he is not like you. He grew up in a time when animals were trophies to be hunted. Not saved. And besides, we thought we were rescuing you."

'And then?" April asked. "Because someone obviously stopped him from shooting Bear. Was it you?"

Tör had the grace to blush. "Not me. Not at first, anyway."

"*Who*, then?"

She didn't notice the footsteps until her father suddenly appeared next to Tör, and like Tör, he rubbed his eyes and couldn't stop gawking at the pair of them.

"You?" she said incredulously. "You saved Bear?"

She stared at him as if seeing him for the first time. With his tweed jacket, wild hair, and scent of aniseed, he still looked like Dad—and yet, at the same time, somehow he looked different. As if the flimsy parchment shell around him had finally dissolved and a solid flesh-and-blood version had appeared in his place.

"Dad," she said, grinning, "this is Bear."

He stepped forward clumsily and stuck out a hand. "Pleased to meet you . . . Bear."

Bear took one look at the outstretched hand and bared his teeth. Dad retreated hastily backward. "He's only saying thank you," April said, and then threw her arms around Dad. "I'm saying thank you too."

When April eventually let go, Dad's hair was even more messed up than usual, but there was a smile on his face that she hadn't seen for years.

"So—you believe me now?" she said. "I was trying to rescue him! So he could go home—back to Svalbard to be with the other polar bears."

"April," Dad said, taking off his glasses and looking at her carefully, "I should have believed you all along."

"But you didn't. You said I was making him up."

"And I was wrong," he said softly.

April nodded and tried to smile back. But it was hard. There was a lump in her throat, and she didn't trust herself to speak.

"You know why I love Mozart?" Dad asked, clearing his throat with a gruff cough. "He was one of the greatest composers who ever lived. Not because he wrote music with his head, but because he wrote music from his heart. And when you live from your heart, it's impossible to ever tell a lie." He paused to wipe something from his eye that might or might not have been a tear. "I . . . should have known you were telling the truth because, April, my dear girl, you're just like your mother and your heart never lies."

That was when he took her hand in his, albeit

awkwardly, and squeezed. And it was also when April realized she had gotten her father back. She realized a lot of other things too, which rushed in and out of her head like skippy, fluttering butterflies.

But she didn't have time to think about them, because Bear drowned out all those thoughts with a roar. The kind of roar that made the ship shudder, the sea rock, and lives shift and change. Then he looked from one to the other with a smile that looked like cotton candy and sunshine mixed together.

"He's happy," said April to a shocked Tör and a bemused Dad. "Would you like to hear my roar too?"

Just as she was preparing to let out the biggest roar ever, the door to the cargo hold crashed open and the captain appeared, holding a rifle in his hands pointed directly at Bear.

"NO!" April flung herself in front of Bear. "Don't shoot!"

Dad hurriedly stepped forward so he was now in

front of both Bear and April. "He's quite safe, sir," he said in a calm, measured voice. "My daughter has him completely under control. You can put the gun down."

"Are you crazy?" the captain said, tightening his grip. "You can't control a wild polar bear!"

"No," said April. "*You* can't. But I can."

The captain's face wore all the emotion of the sea at its fiercest, but this time, April wasn't afraid—not with Bear by her side and bear courage in her heart. And so she stretched herself to her full height and looked the captain straight in the eye. "He's my best friend, and I don't expect anyone who doesn't like animals to understand that. But you all saw how he saved my life." She stepped closer to Bear and curled an arm around his neck. "If you kill him, you have to kill me first."

"And me," said Dad, putting his own arm around April.

"And me," said Tör, who April had forgotten was

there at all, but who positioned himself in front of all of them.

"Son?" The captain lowered his rifle. "You believe this?"

"Dad," Tör replied, pulling himself up straight. "You were the one who taught me that the ocean is a world of mystery that man can never hope to fully understand. Even if that means a girl can be friends with a polar bear. So yes, I do believe it."

The captain looked at Tör, his weathered face torn between what his son was asking of him and his duty to the ship. April held her breath.

"Times have changed," continued Tör in a gentler voice. "Maybe it is time for us to change too."

"Okay, okay," the captain said at last, albeit grudgingly. "But what are we supposed to do? Take the bear to the nearest zoo?"

"Bear doesn't belong in a zoo!" April shouted. "We have to take him back to Svalbard!"

The captain looked at her as if she had gone mad.

"Bear Island was once full of bears," she explained. "That's why it was called Bear Island in the first place! Now there aren't any left. You know why? Because the ice caps have melted, and they can't get there anymore. That's why we have to take him home."

"And this is my responsibility because?"

"Because it's all our responsibility!" April cried. "Don't you see? It's not you, or me, who's melted the ice caps. It's *all* of us. And if we don't do what we can to help, then very soon there won't be any polar bears left."

"Dad." Tör turned to his father. "She's right. And it's not just about the polar bears. You said yourself many times the sea ice is retreating farther and farther each year. We are seeing it with our own eyes."

"You want me to save every polar bear I see?"

"No," April said. "Just this one."

"You think I don't wish to save the Arctic too?" the

captain said in exasperation. "But it needs more than a little girl rescuing one polar bear."

"I agree," said April. "But imagine if *every single person* on the planet just did one thing."

"Then it is still not enough."

"But it's better than doing nothing."

The captain looked contemplatively at them and seemed to be wrestling with something deep inside himself—it was the longest of times before he spoke. "I have sailed these waters for over thirty years, and it is true I have seen the ice caps melt in my own lifetime faster than I ever would have believed possible." He glanced sideways at Tör with a thoughtful expression. "Soon, the Arctic I knew will not be the Arctic my son will know. I am not just doing this for you. I am doing this for him."

April grabbed hold of Bear's paw in delight and couldn't stop the beam of joy that shimmied through her body.

"But I won't have him hurting any of the crew under my watch. He stays chained up at all times, do you understand?"

She nodded.

And with that, the ship headed north.

28

SVALBARD

SVALBARD WAS a stealer of breath.

It shone like diamonds in the sun. It danced under skies so huge, they seemed bottomless. It glistened and breathed and sang its own kind of magic. They had sailed into the main port at Longyearbyen, the capital of Svalbard and the world's northernmost settlement of any kind. It was a place of final frontiers and unimaginable adventures, and one of the last places on Earth that still ached with pure, deep, still wilderness.

April had stayed in the hold the entire voyage, glued to Bear's side, and it was only now that the ship had docked in the port with a loud thud, and that everyone had disembarked, excluding the captain, that Bear was unchained and allowed to be brought on deck.

April felt her breath leave her body in a rush. Svalbard was the most beautiful place she had ever seen. So close to the North Pole, the air smelled of ice, something clean and pure and dreamlike. Beside her, Bear quivered.

"This is it," she said. "Do you remember?"

Bear cocked his head in response. His eyes brightened, and what seemed like a smile passed across his face. As if acting purely from instinct, he started to move down the gangplank toward the shore, and April scurried to keep up.

Lisé waited for them on shore, a young woman with purple hair and a French accent. She wore a red rain jacket, rainbow boots, and a huge grin. April, who had been wearing some of Tör's castoffs, liked her immediately.

"So you're the girl who saved the polar bear." Lisé

gazed at her in awe. "Everyone here is talking about you!"

April blushed. "I just did what I had to."

"I understand that." Lisé spanned her arms to include the beautiful but endangered surroundings. "That's why we're all here. Doing our bit. Now, this must be your lovely Bear?"

Bear had paused on the gangplank and was sniffing the air curiously. There was just one step to take before he was home. In the faint breeze, something rustled and moved, and the scent of other polar bears wafted back. April could smell them. Something musky, feral, and alive.

"Oh, he's a beauty, isn't he?" Lisé said. "He'll be in safe hands here."

Tör had told her all about the Polar Institute on the way, explaining that it was a Norwegian government organization that was doing its best to protect and conserve the area around Svalbard.

"We'll keep an eye on him just to make sure he's fully fit and healthy after his journey."

April nodded.

"You did a very brave thing," Lisé said gently. "Not necessarily in the right way. But he belongs here."

Under her hand, Bear's heart raced and danced. He still had that final step to take until he actually stood ashore on Svalbard, but his entire body was coiled and poised. April's chest thudded. "But I don't know if I'm ready!" she cried, her fingers finding the soft place behind his ear. "I wish I could stay with him."

"I'm sure he does too." Lisé smiled. "You've had an amazing adventure. Go home, share your story with everyone who wants to listen and especially to those who don't, and do what you can to tell everyone about us up here in Svalbard. The Arctic needs everyone's help more than ever before."

Behind her, the ship's horn blared, and April jumped. She had been so caught up in Bear, she hadn't even noticed people had starting boarding. The captain had to turn the ship back around. She had known they were only stopping briefly. But not this briefly. Time was running away from her, and she felt breathless trying to catch up.

"He likes to be stroked behind his left ear," she said quickly. "And when he's happy, he rolls on his back and wants his tummy rubbed. And here." She thrust out the last remaining jar of peanut butter that Dad had retrieved from the storeroom. "He loves this."

Lisé took the jar and held it tight. "I will do my very best to look after him as well as you have done. But remember that he is a wild animal. I suspect that once he is back with his kind, he won't need human contact anymore." She studied April thoughtfully. "Indeed, it is highly unusual to have such a bond with a wild polar bear. I have never seen anything quite like it."

April didn't trust herself to speak, so she nodded.

"Would you like a photo before you go? Of the pair

of you? I can email it to you."

Lisé had a digital camera for the high-resolution pictures they posted on their website, and she pointed it toward them. Bear reared onto his hind legs like the brilliant white stallion he was and wrapped one paw gently around her shoulders, and she leaned into his embrace.

When it was taken—a flash of white that made her blink—Lisé held out her hands in goodbye. "I think your ship is ready," she said as the ship's horn blasted once more, and then, giving April space, she melted back toward the conservation center.

In front of her only Bear remained.

"Well, Bear. It's time."

Her heart quickened, and under her palm, Bear's heart quickened too. For the first time since arriving, he turned his attention away from Svalbard and back to April.

"Bear?" She squared his face in her hands so they were gazing at each other. His chocolate eyes twinkled, melted, and poured into her own. She blinked a few times so she could see him clearly. "We've been through a few adventures together, but you're home now, aren't you?" April whispered. "You can sense it. I can tell. And . . . now I have to go home too."

Bear whimpered and let out a low, painful moan that made her heart throb. He nudged her face until she put her arms around him.

April rested her face against his cheek. "But you'll be okay here. Look! You're in safe hands. Lisé is lovely. She said you're wild, but if you ever do need some strokes and cuddles, then you just come to her, okay? And I'll send you some peanut butter through the mail, but don't eat too much—otherwise you'll get fat."

Bear's ears twitched as the two friends leaned closely into each other. The ship's horn blew once more. Time rushed and sped and shortened. Racing as fast as her heart. She tightened her grip, kissed him a thousand times, and felt something inside her break.

"I love you, Bear."

And with that, she finally let go.

29

THE LAST ROAR

WHILE BEAR WAS TAKING his first steps back onto the land where he belonged, April's ship slowly started to sail away from Svalbard. She stood on deck, pinned to the rear, with her arms and hands stretched out over the sea in goodbye. On the shore, Bear gazed after the ship in confusion. He was an animal, after all, and didn't entirely know why she was leaving him behind.

"Bear!" she cried as if her whole heart was broken. "Bear!"

By now the ship was traveling faster, leaving a wake of white waves behind it, speeding farther and farther

away. And all the time, Bear was growing smaller and smaller on the shore.

"BEAR!" she screamed from the very depths of her being. "BEAR!"

The pain rose up from somewhere she didn't even know existed. It rocketed up like a wave and rolled over her like thunder. There was a rip somewhere in the chasm of the universe. Something splintering in a thousand trillion pieces. And she knew however hard she searched, she would never be able to find them all again.

How could she live without him?

How?

It wasn't even a question, because there was no answer. It was a cry from the very deepest part of her being, the part of her that she hadn't even known existed until now, but that had always been there.

It was as if her own soul was being ripped from her.

How could she be happy never stroking him again?

Never being able to sink her face into his soft fur? Never seeing his ears twitch? Never seeing the grin on his face as he rolled and squirmed on his back in the sun? Never feeling his wet nose on her skin? Or his tongue licking her freckles? Never seeing him bound out of the sea? Never riding on his back and climbing mountains and feeling like she was the happiest, most loved girl on Earth?

How could time just tick on and Bear *not* be part of her life?

"I can't!" she sobbed. "I can't live without him."

The grief was so huge, so monstrous, so ugly, she could barely swallow. She could still see him. Growing smaller. Not her giant-sized Bear. But someone smaller and smaller. Too small! Disappearing before her eyes.

"Bear!" she cried again, her voice hoarse with pain. "BEAR!"

On the shore—she could just about still see him—

Bear rose up on his hind legs, and his mouth opened in one last cavernous roar. It spun and danced and raced across the waves. It scrambled across the water, chasing the boat, and finally it reached her.

Bear's roar.

Bear's *last* roar.

She clasped it with both hands; she clasped it as if it was the most precious thing in the whole wide world, she clasped it as if she would never let go. And as the tears streamed down her face, she watched Bear disappear from sight for the very last time.

"It's all right. He's safe now." A gentle hand rested on her elbow. "April, my girl. My precious, dear girl."

She spun around and burrowed her face into her father's tweed jacket, which had never felt so familiar or so comforting. She stayed there a very long time with her dad stroking her hair as she cried—so hard she could barely breathe, and her eyes were sore and red and swollen. But eventually her sobs subsided into little hiccups, her breathing settled, and Dad was able to pass her his hankie to blow her nose.

"He'll be okay, won't he?"

"You saved him, April." Dad crouched down so he was her height. "Now he can have a life. A genuine polar bear life."

"But . . ." April took a deep, shuddery breath. "What if he can't get used to being around the other bears?"

"Isn't this what he wanted?" Dad peered into her face. "To be back where he belonged? To not be stuck alone on the island anymore?"

"Yes," she answered in a small voice.

"You've returned him to his true home so he can survive. I think he'll be happy, don't you?"

She gulped and swallowed back the tears. "But . . . what about me?"

"He won't ever forget you, April Wood," Dad replied. "How could he? You saved his life."

"I didn't mean that."

"What, then?"

"How will *I* be happy?" She blinked back the tears. "You've never gotten over . . ."

Dad took a sharp intake of breath. "Your mother, you mean?" He sighed deeply. "Because grown-ups can be quite blind sometimes. I have the most wonderful, brave-hearted daughter right under my nose, and from now on, we are going to be a real family and I am going to be a real father."

April tried to muster up a smile, but the most that would come was a hiccup.

"How do you feel about moving to the seaside to be near Granny Apples? We can find a nice cottage and you can start at one of those friendly-looking local schools."

"But what about your work at the university?"

"I'm going to hand in my notice," he said. "I thought I . . . might try to apply for a job at one of the universities down there. I hear one of them is looking for people to come up with a compostable solution to plastic."

"You'll be good at that," April said, thinking of how smart he was, and then patted his arm. "That *is* doing."

"And we'll spend more time together," he said, smiling at her with eyes that twinkled like stars. "I promise."

As April gazed up at him, she realized Dad wasn't just speaking with words. He was actually speaking with all the unspoken things that make words mean something special, and her spirits lifted in response. Living near Granny Apples and the seaside sounded lovely, and though her stomach felt like lead at the thought of leaving the Arctic without Bear, at least she was leaving with a real father.

"I will send you photos when we next visit," Tör said. She hadn't even noticed he was there. She couldn't imagine what she looked like. Red-faced, blotchy, and covered in snot. But she didn't care.

"You will?"

"Of course," Tör said. "I will send you as many pictures as you want. I will send you so many pictures, you will be able to make wallpaper out of them."

"I would like that," April said. "I would like that very much."

"And maybe one day you can come back," Tör said with a blue-eyed smile.

"Oh," she said. "I will. I'm definitely coming back. And when I'm old enough, I'm going to move here and work at the Polar Institute."

"Somehow," said Tör, "I don't doubt you."

"After all," said April, lifting herself to her full height and looking out to sea, "someone's got to save the polar bears."

With that, she opened her mouth and roared.

And because she had learned to roar a real polar bear roar—not just a little girl's roar—and because she had saved the best roar for last, it traveled and danced and skipped over the waves all the way to Svalbard. Bear was still waiting on the shore. Standing on his two rear legs like a brilliant white stallion. His ears pricked. His nose twitched, and his eyes were watering either with the wind or something else. When her roar finally came, bouncing and skipping across the waves, it landed right at his feet. He stood for a moment and allowed the roar to envelop him in one last April-sized hug. It was the biggest, best hug of all. Then he dropped to all fours and bounded off to join his new life.

AUTHOR'S NOTE

The real Bear Island is almost, but not exactly, as depicted in this book. Geographically and dimensionally it is the same, and it is true that it is uninhabited save for a weather station. However, on the real Bear Island, the weather station is run by a team of eleven rather than a father and daughter. (And I'm also fairly sure their methods of reading the weather are a lot more scientific than those I have described!) Any work of fiction has to somehow mold the setting around the story, so I took some liberty with the island's topography and a few other aspects to fit the narrative. There really is a Walrus Bay—I didn't make that one up—and even as remote as Bear Island is, there is still a surprising amount of washed-up plastic on its beaches. Apart from that, any mistakes are purely my own, and I apologize in advance.

And of course, I took some liberties with the character of Bear. As cuddly as he is, polar bears in real life are extremely dangerous wild animals, and I would never advise trying to actually befriend one.

But there is something incredibly special about a polar bear. So it comes as no surprise that they are often called the poster child of climate change—because as the Arctic warms at double the rate of the rest of the planet, they are sadly bearing the biggest brunt. Even more sadly, according to the International Union for Conservation of Nature (IUCN) it is predicted that the polar bear population will be in serious decline by 2050.

There is some dispute over exactly how much and how quickly the sea ice is melting. This is because it expands and contracts with the seasons and isn't the easiest thing to measure. But NASA records over a forty-two-year satellite period show that the Arctic has lost just over a million square miles of sea ice. Another statistic put the decline at over 12 percent per decade, with the most pronounced winter reduction in the Svalbard and Barents Sea area.

Finally, here are a few resources I used in my research, which I thought you might find interesting too:

You can read about the World Wildlife Fund here—what they are doing to help polar bears and other endangered species, and how you can help:

www.worldwildlife.org

The Polar Institute really does exist, and you can read about it here:

www.npolar.no/en

If you want to read up on Bear Island, I found this website very useful, and it has some photographs of the weather station and Walrus Bay (Kvalrossbukta):

www.spitsbergen-svalbard.com/spitsbergen-information /islands-svalbard-co/bjornoya.html

You can also go to Google Maps and have a look at it for yourself.

ACKNOWLEDGMENTS

From the very first moment I met the team at Harper-Collins, I knew they were the perfect home not just for Bear but for me too. So, a huge roar-like thank-you to Renée Cafiero, Gwen Morton, Audrey Diestelkamp, Emma Meyer, Alison Klapthor, and Louisa Currigan, and special thanks to Kate Slater for her beautiful cover and illustrations.

To my two amazing editors—Erica Sussman and Harriet Wilson—heartfelt thanks for making my dreams come true. I am so immensely grateful for your unswerving support, your love of Bear, and your belief in me. (And I still can't quite believe this is all happening!)

To my dream agent, Claire Wilson, thank you for changing my life in the course of one joy-filled email. I am so happy to have you on my side.

My parents have always supported me in more ways than one. We are not a family who say "I love you," but I really do. To Jonathan and Nicki; my brother-in-law, Peter, who keeps telling me "this is just the beginning" (I hope so because I've got lots more stories to tell!); Connor; my aunts and uncles on both sides—including Chris's—and our adopted American family friend, Marilyn McKnight. Thank you also to those who aren't here but I know are still cheering me on from the other side, including my grandparents and my beloved father-in-law. And because my stories wouldn't exist if I didn't love animals, to my adored cat, Gremmie, for all my furry cuddles, and our pet tortoise, Arthur, for helping me not take life too seriously.

If I didn't mention my husband, I don't think he would ever speak to me again, so a huge, huge thank-you to Chris. Meeting you under that orange tree was the best thing that ever happened to me and a story of its own. You are my biggest champion and the best husband I ever could have wished for.

Of course, I cannot write these acknowledgments without thanking Bear. To be trusted with his story has been the most amazing privilege I have ever had. You grew in my heart and filled the void I didn't even know I had. You're out in the big wide world now, and I hope that my readers grow to love you just as much as I do. (But please don't feed him too much peanut butter, okay?) You represent not just one bear but polar bears everywhere who need our love and protection more than ever. And you demonstrate that the connection between humans and animals is only a heartbeat apart.

And finally, my dear readers, this book is ultimately for you! We live in a world that is changing fast, and sometimes this can feel frightening. But I hope you take strength from April's story, I hope you keep seeing the beauty of our beautiful planet, and I thank you from the bottom of my heart for reading my book. It means so very much to me.

Turn the page for a sneak peek at

The Lost Whale

By Hannah Gold

CHAPTER ONE

ARRIVAL

The first thing Rio Turner noticed when he stepped into the arrivals hall of Los Angeles International Airport was the noise. Airports were never destined to be quiet places and this gigantic, sprawling monster was like a football stadium in full roar.

The second thing he noticed was his grandmother.

Even though it had been five years since he'd last seen her, Rio recognized her straight away. She towered over everyone in a shiny turquoise jumpsuit, wore thick, black-rimmed glasses and had a shock of white wiry hair.

Gazing around, it took a few moments for her to

register him. "Rio?" she asked. "It is you, isn't it?" She paused in front of him. "I barely recognized you. You're so . . ."

Her voice tailed off and Rio wondered what she'd been about to say. Either way, he wasn't going to ask. Instead, he crossed his arms protectively against his chest.

"You made it then." She hurried on, her eyes full of something he didn't recognize. "I am *so* glad you're here."

Then she enveloped him in a hug.

Not the kind of hug he was used to—deep, warm, and snuggly. It was all hard angles and sharp elbows and smelled of peppermints. Rio counted to three before he could bear it no longer. Then he yanked himself away.

"Rio?" she asked falteringly, two bright spots of color on her cheeks. "It's been a long time and I know all this must seem impossibly strange to you right now, but I want you to feel at home while you're staying with me. I am your grandmother after all."

Rio, who had been staring at the floor during the latter part of her speech, looked up in surprise. She had signed Christmas and birthday cards *from Grandma*, but he couldn't think of anyone who looked less like a grandmother than her. Not compared to his other grandma anyway, who wore thick, rubber-soled slippers and loved to call him "ducky" even though the last time he'd checked, he hadn't yet grown a beak and feathers. No, this person didn't feel like a grandmother at all and he secretly resolved to call her by her first name, Fran, instead.

When he didn't answer, she rubbed her hands together despite the fact that it wasn't cold. "Well, I guess we better make a move."

Refusing her offer to carry his suitcase—he was perfectly capable of that himself—Rio followed her toward the exit where, in the parking zone, she halted by a 4 x 4 covered in a thick coating of dust.

He climbed into the passenger seat, pulled his seatbelt across his body, and chewed his lip, trying to ignore the sudden, desperate urge for a wee.

As if sensing his discomfort, Fran turned to face him and seemed about to say something. But again, whatever it was died on her lips. Instead, she just cleared her throat. "I'm . . . sorry about your mother."

Rio felt the sudden hot sting of tears and rubbed his eyes furiously, hoping she hadn't seen. To avoid any further conversation, he stared out of the window and after a brief pause, she switched on the engine with a rough twist of the key, and they were off.

California was the place where Rio's mother had been born and where she grew up. She'd left when she was barely twenty, first on a music scholarship to New York and then, upon graduation, as a violinist in the London Philharmonic Orchestra. In all that time, she'd only been back once, taking Rio with her when he was just a tiny baby.

So long ago, he couldn't remember any of it.

But technically, by virtue of his mother's birth, he was half-American. Although it was a very small half because he'd lived in London all eleven-and-a-quarter years of his life and spoke with a decidedly English accent. And so, this exotic, faraway world of endless sunshine, tall fluttering palm trees, and golden beaches had always felt like a dream. And in truth, Rio had been looking forward to coming back nearly all his life.

Just not like this.

Opening the car window, he took a deep gulp of the Californian air. Unfortunately, this wasn't the cleverest thing to do on a highway. Rio coughed and spluttered and felt the smog on his lungs.

This was California?

Everything was so *big* here. The cars, the road signs,

the buildings—even the sky, looping above their heads in a vast indigo silence. As if the car had been picked up and thrown into a world full of giants. London was a city, but it didn't feel anything like *this*.

Mom had always said that California was different. That it was peaceful. That its temperament would suit Rio. That . . .

He closed the window with a snap. Then, ignoring his grandmother's attempts at conversation, he shut his eyes and tried to pretend he was still in a universe where his mother hadn't sent him away to the other side of the world to stay with someone he barely even knew.

CHAPTER TWO

OCEAN BAY

At some point, Rio must have fallen asleep because the next thing he knew the car had ground to a halt. "We're here," his grandmother said. "Welcome to Ocean Bay."

Dusk had stolen in, and he had to blink a few times to make sure he was seeing properly. The small coastal town of Ocean Bay was about an hour north of LA. Not that he could spot the town right now. His grandmother lived on the outskirts and the moon shone down on a huge, rambling beach house made of wood. It was a higgledy-piggledy-shaped building three stories high and painted top to toe in a soft pastel green.

...ce, Rio felt his insides soften. As if the
... had magic healing properties and could smooth
away even the most jagged of edges.

He rubbed his eyes. The apartment he shared with
his mother was so small it could probably squeeze
itself into this house half a dozen times over.

"It's beautiful, isn't it?" Fran murmured, a note of
pride in her voice.

But if he thought the house was special, when Rio
stepped out of the car the noise was something else
entirely. A magnificent, almighty roar. The kind of
noise only something extraordinarily powerful could
make.

It was the roar of the ocean.

And Rio, who didn't even like loud noises, discovered to his surprise that this noise was different. He
could feel the force of it coursing through his body
and had a sudden intense desire to suck the feeling
right down to his belly and dislodge the tight band of

pain trapped in his chest.

"Plenty of time for you to explore the beach." Fran beckoned him from the front step. "Come inside for now."

He reluctantly followed her through the wide-open hallway and into the kitchen, where unlike back home, there were no photos, school drawings, or any shopping lists tacked untidily to the wall. There weren't even any dirty mugs or discarded plates or half-eaten ginger biscuits. Instead, the room was full of cool, steel appliances that gleamed so brightly he could see his reflection in them—a thin, pale-faced boy with a guarded expression and a thatch of unruly light brown hair that never looked neat no matter how much he brushed it. The only sign of color was his favorite yellow t-shirt—the one Mom had bought him for his last birthday.

After a few moments, Fran placed a steaming plate of food in front of him. "Vegetable chili. I made it

...i my own secret recipe. Eat up now."

...-t-thank you," Rio replied, hating the way his voice wobbled whenever he felt nervous. The only things he knew about his grandmother were that she was once a principal, she'd lived in Ocean Bay all her life, and that she spoke with an American accent.

As he ate, she chattered away from the other side of the kitchen. "I thought tomorrow I could give you a tour of Ocean Bay," she said. "Maybe we can go shopping or, or . . . perhaps I could show you the marina or even take you to the lighthouse! Up there you can see for miles and miles. It's quite the sight. Or, if you're feeling tired, we could just take a walk along the beach together?"

She looked expectantly at him over her glasses.

The words Rio really wanted to say remained stuck in his throat. That he hadn't come here to have fun or go shopping and he most definitely hadn't come here to spend time with someone who hadn't even been part of his life when he'd needed her the most.

Luckily his grandmother was distracted by the entrance of a long-haired white cat with a black patch of fur over its left eye who announced its presence with a plaintive meow. "Pirate! There you are! Would you like to meet our guest?"

The cat didn't seem particularly bothered about getting to know Rio, but nevertheless something in his chest softened. He'd always wanted a pet—even just a hamster—but the apartment rules had forbidden it. He leaned down to stroke the cat behind its ears and was rewarded with a loud purr.

"This is my grandson, Rio. He's come all the way from London to stay with us for a vacation. Do you want to say hello?"

Rio wasn't sure if it was the silly voice she used to speak to Pirate—the kind grown-ups put on for babies—or the fact that he was exhausted after a twelve-hour plane journey, or how she used the

...rd for *holiday*. Maybe it was everything.

...way, the words burst out of his chest before he
...ould stop them. "It's not a *vacation*! I'm not here for
fun! I'm only here because I have to be!"

Fran opened and then closed her mouth. Rio
thought she was going to say something, but she just
shooed Pirate off the table and then busied herself
with removing strands of white fur from her jumpsuit.

The rest of the meal passed in silence.